Gabi
~~A Gordita~~
~~A Fatgirl~~
A Girl in Pieces

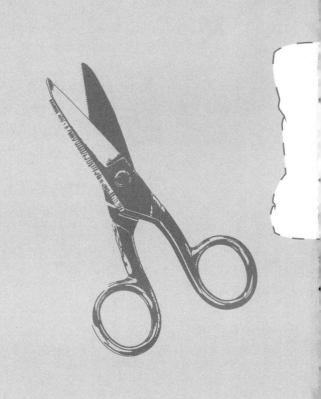

Gabi

A ~~Gordita~~

A ~~Fatgirl~~

A Girl in Pieces

BY

ISABEL QUINTERO

an imprint of Lee & Low Books Inc.
New York

Text copyright © 2014 by Isabel Quintero
Cover and interior illustrations copyright © 2014 by Zeke Peña
Illustrations inspired by collages by Isabel Quintero

Design by Zeke Peña
Production by The Kids at Our House
The text is set in Officina Sans ITC Std Book
Manufactured in the United States of America
by Lake Book Manufacturing, LLC
(hc) 10 9 8 7 6 5 4 3   (pb) 23 22 21 20 19 18 17 16
First edition

Library of Congress Cataloging-in-Publication Data
Quintero, Isabel.
  Gabi, a girl in pieces / by Isabel Quintero. — First edition.
     pages cm
  Summary: Sixteen-year-old Gabi Hernandez chronicles her senior year in high school as she copes with her friend Cindy's pregnancy, friend Sebastian's coming out, her father's meth habit, her own cravings for food and cute boys, and especially the poetry that helps forge her identity.
  ISBN 978-1-935955-94-8 (hardback : alk. paper) —ISBN 978-1-935955-95-5 (pbk. : alk. paper) —ISBN 978-1-935955-96-2 (e-book)
  [1. High schools—Fiction. 2. Schools—Fiction. 3. Pregnancy—Fiction. 4. Gays—Fiction. 5. Family problems—Fiction. 6. Mexican Americans—Fiction.] I. Title.
  PZ7.Q438Gab 2014
  [Fic]—dc23   2014007658

EN PRIMERO:
para la persona who first read to me and taught
me that words mattered and changed you.

Gracias, Mamá.

Y EN SEGUNDO:
for all the gorditas, flaquitas, and
in-between girls trying to make their space in
the world.

Don't worry, you got this.

—ISABEL QUINTERO

Gabi

July 24

My mother named me Gabriela after my grandmother who—coincidentally—didn't want to meet me when I was born because my mother was not married and was therefore living in sin. My mom has told me the story many, many, MANY times of how, when she confessed to my grandmother that she was pregnant with me, her mother beat her. BEAT HER! She was twenty-five.

That story forms the basis of my sexual education.

Every time I go out with a guy, my mom says, "Ojos abiertos, piernas cerradas." Eyes open, legs closed. That's as far as the birds and the bees talk has gone. And I don't mind it. I don't necessarily agree with that whole wait-until-you're-married crap though. I mean, this is America and the twenty-first century, not Mexico one hundred years ago. But, of course, I can't tell my mom that because she'll think I'm bad.

Or worse: trying to be White.

July 25

Less than a month before school starts again. Ugh. It's not like I don't want to go back to school (because I do), but I also want to lie around and do nothing for a little bit longer. Eat some tacos. Eat a few more Rocky

Road ice cream cones from Rite-Aid so I have an excuse to talk to the really cute guy there who has a full sleeve but has to cover it up because apparently Rite-Aid keeps it classy. Not like he's asked me for my number but, hey, at least I can say he's given me something sweet.

What I really want to do before summer vacation is over is try the new super-hot wings from Pepe's House of Wings, located—conveniently—down the street. The wings are rumored to be so hot that you have to sign a waiver before you put one little drumstick in your mouth. Which makes me wonder, what horrible thing happens when you eat them? Could you possibly have a heart attack from ingesting so much capsaicin? (I like that word. It makes me feel scientific.) DEATH BY DIGESTING FIERY WING. Sounds borderline mythical. Maybe you stop breathing but are on such a spicy-wing high that it doesn't matter because it's the best thing you've ever eaten and it's like there are angels lifting you into heaven while your mouth burns away here on earth.

But, with my luck, I'd probably just get the runs.

Right now though, I seriously have to get up and clean my room before my mom sees the little treasures under my pillow. That woman is always finding my stash.

July 25

Later the same afternoon...

Okay. So I met up with Cindy and Sebastian and we had the wings at Pepe's House of Wings. But my best friends are weaklings when it comes to spicy food and only ate barbecue and lemon pepper wings. Chickens. I, however, ate the super spicy (aka Caliente Caliente) wings. It felt so good signing that waiver, like I was about to do something so epic, so courageous, so dangerous, and so for the benefit of all human kind that I would be willing to sign my life away to do it. Of course it would be just like me that the most dangerous thing I have done up to this moment would be food related. *Ugh*.

Note to self: lose some weight. It is senior year, after all.

July 25

Later...

I was right. I got the runs.

July 28

What the fuck just happened?

Long day. Have to sleep.

July 29

Yesterday was unreal. Cindy called me and told me that she needed me to come over because she had to tell me something. Last time one of my friends said they had to tell me something was when Sebastian told me he was gay. He called me and said he had "something" to tell me. Not that I didn't know. I mean, I've known him since the third grade and he's always been gay. But I was happy that he finally came out, to me at least. It was funny too. He took me to Denny's and said, "Gabi, I have something to tell you." And I was like, *Oh my God, he's gonna tell me he's gay*. And he was like, "Ugh, I can't say it." So he wrote, "I'm gay" on a napkin and passed it to me. I looked at it and couldn't help whispering, "I know." We both kind of laughed and were relieved.

Now he just has to tell his parents.

But when Cindy said she had something to tell me, I was wondering how I would react if she told me she was a lesbian. It would be super weird, wouldn't it? I mean, we've gotten dressed in front of each other, gone skinny dipping in her pool. Should I be concerned about that? I doubt it. Not that I thought she would be checking me out (a lot) because, really, who checks out the fat girl?

Cindy didn't tell me she was a lesbian though—which really would have been easier to handle after I found out what the "something" was.

The something was that she might be pregnant.

PREGNANT? Really? What the hell?! I mean I didn't even know she had had sex. Or that she had a boyfriend. What kind of best friends for life are we? The kind that don't share such intimacies, I guess. (I hope I used the word intimacies correctly. I need to get back into school mode.) Anyway, I was so pissed at the situation. Pissed and disappointed. Not at the fact that she had sex, but that she hadn't been careful. That she had just become another statistic: Hispanic Teen Mom #3,789,258. Or some ridiculous actual number that we had been lectured about last year and had sworn we would never become. We had even criticized the girls who showed and called them stupid. "When we have sex, we'll use a condom." We had been so sure about it.

Our conversation was something like this:

ME: (sitting comfortably and spinning around in her desk chair) Hola muchacha! What is so urgent I had to leave a pack of half-eaten Oreos behind hidden in my underwear drawer?

CINDY: I saw...IT.

ME: *It?* That stupid movie about the clown who's really a spider? I know. We watched it together.

CINDY: No. It. It. You know, a boy's *It*?

ME: (no longer spinning around in Cindy's desk chair) Wha...? What do you mean? Please tell me you mean a boy's clown movie? Because you can't mean penis. You can't mean THAT.

She looked at me with tears in her eyes, threw herself on the bed and started crying. I was in shock.

ME: (In my best I-am-here-for-you-best-friend-even-though-you-just-did-something-really-stupid voice) It's okay. It's okay. Please stop crying. Just tell me what happened.

CINDY: I went to a party with German a few weeks after we got out of school and I got drunk and then we did it in his car and I haven't gotten my period! What am I going to do?

ME: What?

CINDY: Oh my God! Aren't you listening?

ME: Yes. I almost wish I wasn't, to tell you the truth. You went to a party, got drunk, and fucked German. I was listening. But you never told me any of this. Ever.

Now I started to cry. Not only because I was hurt about her not telling me, but because I knew that she had just fucked up her future in a major fucked-up way.

CINDY: I didn't tell you because I knew you would be mad. Would be like, "Why are you going out with that idiot? Why are you going to a party at Sandra's? Why are you drinking?" And you know what? You're right! I shouldn't have gone but I did. I did! What do I do? What if I'm pregnant? I can't have a baby! I don't want to change diapers! My mom is going to kick my ass! Seriously, she'll kill me!

ME: Okay well...(I felt bad for her because her mom probably would kick her ass). You're not even sure if there's a bun in the oven. Maybe you haven't gotten your period because you're stressed? I read somewhere that that can happen.

CINDY: Really? Are you sure? That's probably it then. (She sounded too relieved, so I had to bring her back to reality.)

ME: I didn't say I was sure. I said *maybe*. But to make sure, why don't we go to Stuffix Pharmacy after the SATs on Saturday and get one of those pregnancy tests?

She agreed. After we settled down, got some ice cream and Hot Cheetos, we watched *Juno* and thought about how much Sunny Delight we would have to buy.

July 30

I lay in bed for a long time this morning, thinking about Cindy and the fact that she could be pregnant. I don't like German, she was right about that. He's an idiot. German is one of those guys who knows he's super hot and assumes that girls HAVE to like him. Like, if he asks a girl out and she says no, he's one of those guys who will say stupid things such as, "Well, fuck you, stupid bitch—I was trying to do you a favor." One of those gems. What he doesn't understand is that we don't have to like him. It doesn't matter if you're a beauty queen like Cindy (tall, thin, beautiful olive skin and curly brown hair) or if you're me (short, plump, long straight hair, and super light-skinned), if we don't like you, well, we don't like you.

I don't know how Cindy could've been so stupid as to have sex with him. Anyone but German would have (probably) been better.

The rest of the day I spent arguing with Beto about how loud his music was and that—although I appreciated his love of the Notorious B.I.G.—Rosemary, the little old lady next door (who I love to visit), did not. It didn't matter though, because all I got was a lot of door slamming, volume raising, and "You're not my mom." He's right. I'm just his older sister—but only by two years.

August 1

Saturday. SATs. I woke up late this morning. I had set my alarm for 7:00 a.m., but didn't get up until 7:27. I didn't have time for the bacon and eggs my mom had made, only enough time to kill my dragon-breath with some toothpaste and change into the freshly worn clothes from yesterday. Even then, I barely made it to school in time for the test. Thank God, I can drive now. Otherwise I would have been screwed.

I waited for Cindy after the test and we drove to the pharmacy to face the moment of truth. On the way there, we went through all the possible scenarios. What if she is pregnant? I suggested she tell her mom that an angel had come to her in a dream and told her not to be scared but that she was carrying the son of God. If her mother was as Catholic as she says she is, then she has to believe her. Cindy didn't think it was that funny, but I laughed my ass off!

We walked into the pharmacy. Luckily no one was there. No one except that nosy bitch Georgina. Ugh. And I knew she would have something stupid to say. We got what we needed and went to pay. As luck would have it, she was the only one with a register open. Georgina just smirked at us and said, "Well, Gabi, I know this isn't for you. No one would be fucking your fat ass. So, I guess, the winner is...Cindy! Does German know yet?" (She said this in the most annoying voice possible which—for Georgina—is pretty damn amazing because she already has the most annoying voice possible.)

I don't know what made me say it but I grew some balls at that moment and said, "Your mom would be fucking my fat ass. So shut your trap and do your job, Kmart."

Which, now that I think about it, was an absurd comeback. Why would her mom be fucking my fat ass? Just like me to be saying something dumb like that. Georgina just kept making that stupid face as we walked out of the store.

We went to my house and did the deed.

The stripes turned pink.

We hugged, threw ourselves on my Hello Kitty bedspread, and cried.

August 5

I was sitting at the back of the bus today, watching the old retarded couple making out (like usual), thinking about Cindy, when Georgina got on the bus. As soon as I saw her stupid clown face, I really wished I had begged my mom for at least another hour to let me borrow the car so I could visit Sebastian. I tried to act like I didn't see her and pretended to text but, of course, she sat next to me.

"Hey, fat ass."

"Hola, Little Payasa." She really hates it when I call her that. So I do it as often as I can.

"Look at those two retards. How nasty. People like that should never ever make out. It's so freaking gross!"

I told her she was an idiot and not to say things like that because that was mean, and how does two mentally challenged people loving each other affect her, but talking Georgina out of being an idiot is like making carnitas out of chicken—unnatural. Luckily my stop came by quick, and I was able to leave her behind just as she was beginning to ask about Cindy.

"So how is your prego..."

I made an unkind gesture with my middle finger and stood up.

When I got off the bus, Sebastian was already waiting. He had been gone for a few days with his family on a vacation to Mexico, Mazatlan or somewhere like that near the beach, so he was ultra tan. Right away, I knew he was upset.

"Oh my God! I just talked to Cindy!"

"Did she tell you?"

"Yes!"

"Can you believe that shit?" He shook his head and I said, "Well, she's gone and done it now, and it sucks big hairy ass. But—she wants to keep it. I was there the day she told her mom. For moral support, you know, but it went bad. Really bad. Her mom almost beat the shit out of her. Slapped her hard across the face and asked me to leave. I didn't know what to do, I didn't want to leave her, but her mom went crazy and was yelling at me to go home, and I was afraid that she'd hit me too, so I booked it and left."

We kept going on like that the whole two blocks to his house. When we got there, we locked ourselves in his room. We talked about Cindy forever, and then I finally asked him about his trip. He told me about all the cute boys he saw. His dad let him drink beer with him because apparently in Mexico there is no legal drinking age. Even embryos enjoy a beer with their tacos, he said. I wonder what that would look like? Hmmm. We kept on talking about Mexico and about his grandma who is hilarious and an awesome cook. Sebastian told me about how close he felt to his dad now and that he thought that he would tell him about being gay and that he was sure he would understand. I'm not too sure about that. His dad may be cool with him because they threw back a few beers, but his dad hates gays. I know. I've heard him say it. His exact words were, "I hate pinches jotos." I didn't tell Sebastian though, because I thought it would hurt his feelings. Even if I told him, he would say something like, "It's different because it's me. I'm his son." Yeah, I don't think that would be the case. We talked some more about school and how excited (and nervous) we are that this is our last year and our plans for the future and blah blah blah. It was getting late so I had to leave. He walked me to the bus and waited with me. We heard a car screech to a stop and turned to see what had happened. There was a homeless looking guy on his bike weaving across the street towards us. It was my dad. Luckily the bus showed up before he saw me.

August 7

Sebastian told his parents. He is sleeping on our couch until he finds a permanent home.

August 10

Sebastian hasn't really said anything since his parents dropped him off. They didn't even come in, just dropped him off and threw his stuff on the sidewalk. Cindy came over that night, we watched *Pride and Prejudice*, and my mom ordered us some pizza. She wasn't too happy that Cindy came over though, but she let her stay because she knew that Sebastian needed his friends. Earlier today she had gone on this whole spiel about Cindy's pobrecita madre and the pain that she was going through because of her bad, bad daughter. It was really long. It was something like—

"You can't hang out with her anymore. She is a bad influence. She's a bad, bad girl. I knew that she would come to this. Always so desperate and siempre de ofrecida, no se daba a respetar. No respect for herself at all. What's she gonna do? Quit school? Probably. She can't do both. Maybe she should give up the baby. I don't want you to talk to her anymore. She'll give you bad advice and convince you to do the same thing she did, and then you'll go and open your legs for everybody. You know who I feel sorry for? Her mom. How is Linda going to show her face at parties and church now? Didn't that mensa think about what she would do to her madre? Claro que no! No mas abrio las piernas y ya. Que bonito! Of course not, how nice. But now that she opened her legs and had a good time, the one who is going to have to deal with everything is her mom. Que selfish. Don't even think about calling her or going over there. Her mom is probably feeling really depressed and probably wants to be alone. I'll have to call her and tell her I'm sorry to hear about what happened. Pobrecita Linda, I wonder what she did to deserve such a bad girl? Thank God, you're not like that."

She really has no idea what Cindy is going through. I would have thought that because I was born a bastard child, she would show more sympathy—that she would know how it feels to have your parents react so irrationally. But I guess as you grow older, you forget that you were ever young and that you may have been in love and may have forgotten (or didn't think about) condoms and made mistakes. At least my mom has forgotten. And besides, it's not like Cindy said, "I'm going to sleep with an asshole and get pregnant, just so that my mom can't show her face at parties and my dad won't talk to me. Why? Because I want to be seen as a horrible daughter! Ha, ha, ha!" It was something that happened. I told her that Cindy was not a bad influence, she just made a mistake and that she was my friend, and we had to be there for Sebastian. I argued and begged and she finally said, "Esta bien."

I was surprised that she let Sebastian stay, surprised that she actually felt bad for him. She said that even though she hoped that her own son wouldn't be gay, if he was she would still love him. And that only bad mothers abandon their children. Knowing that made me kind of proud of my mom.

August 15

So we finally found out what happened on the day that Sebastian's parents kicked him out. Apparently his dad said something like, "Odio a los jotos! I hate fags!" (Which must've sounded weird because his dad has a super thick Mexican accent.) "The two worst things that could happen to a man are that his wife sleeps with another man and that his son is gay. And since tu madre querida, ya se habia revolcado with that guy from the laundrymat and is obviously a whore, there was only one more thing left! You ruined my life. Chingado! Hijo de puta! Get out of my house! I don't want to see you ever again. You are no son of mine."

So, yeah, it didn't go as planned. His mom took a telenovela approach to the situation and told him that she would rather be dead than have a gay son and tried to slit her wrists. Obviously she didn't really mean to die or else she would have made sure to pick up a real knife and not a butter knife. I had to hold in a laugh at that. A butter knife, really? Who does that? That very night they told Sebastian that he had to leave, and that's when he called me crying. I woke up my mom and she said it was fine. Even Beto was okay with it. And my brother is not known for his compassion. The only one we didn't tell was my dad but he probably wouldn't have noticed anyway.

Sebastian also told me some other things that made me sad. He told me how he had always known he was gay, but how he had tried to be straight. How he stared at boobs and tried to feel something. How he even pretended to have a crush on Sandra. How he prayed every night, pleading, "Make me love girls, make me love girls," but God didn't listen. I try to imagine Sebastian on his knees, crying and praying and nobody answering.

I wonder how it must feel to have disappointed your mother so much she would rather kill herself than look at you. Never mind—I don't want to know.

August 18

My mom is at it (again), which means my dad finally came back home (and looked like hell). Whenever he comes home after being gone for weeks, with a beard and smelling like he's never heard of a shower, she tries to make our lives seem as normal (whatever that is) as possible. And since Sebastian is here, she's trying as hard as ever. However, all of her attempts make us seem more dysfunctional than before. She came into my room (un-freaking-announced!) and saw me in my underwear! I got super mad and told her to please get out. She was all like, "Ay, I've seen you naked, I'm your mom." But she waited on the other side of my door anyway. When she came in, she had this pink sparkly thing hanging on her arm. I cringed, guessing at what it was. It was a dress. A freakin dress! Ugh! Why does she do that?!?! She knows I hate dresses! How am I going to look in a dress? Ridiculous! Like an overstuffed carne asada burrito, that's how! Beans spilling out the top, tortilla squished together at the bottom. Horrible. Just horrible.

Dresses and I don't get along. The way I see it, a dress is restricting. It's a trap.

Let's say, for example, you are with your friend Cindy at the local elementary school a few blocks from your house and suddenly these really cute boys and one not so cute boy pass by on their bikes. This is just hypothetical, but your friend Cindy thinks it would be funny to flash the boys. Because, you know, she has big boobs, double D's, not like you because not even four of your boobs would equal one of hers and she can do tricks too, she can make them move up and down without even touching them. They have a life of their own, her boobs do.

So, she does it. She really does it! (Even though you thought she was just shitting you!) Shirt goes up and "Hello, boys!" You laugh but since you are laughing so hard you're about to piss your pants, you realize too late that the boys are pedaling back and have decided to do a little flashing of their own. They are coming at you quick with their hands on their zippers! And in an instant, you're in OH-SHIT mode. So now you have to run because maybe you have seen a penis in a picture, or you imagine what it looks like, or they showed a movie once in class about the Holocaust and you were like, "Wow. That's what it looks like. It's uglier than I imagined." But to be confronted with the real thing was not in your plans for a sunny Saturday afternoon.

How does this relate to a dress? Well, hypothetically, you decided to wear a dress and suddenly you have to run home before José whips *It* out, and the shortest route home is to jump Mrs. Sanchez' fence and then jump the other fence to your backyard, and you realize much too late that you are wearing a flouncy brown dress, and you say fuck it and jump the fence anyway, but much to your chagrin only you and half a dress would make the journey. You sneak into your room bare-assed and sweaty—and laugh until your side hurts.

Or if that is not enough reason for hating dresses, what about that time...

...when I was in eighth grade and was walking home and heard a group of boys whistling and laughing. The blonde one shouted, "I can see your underwear!" But I didn't get it. See, I was wearing clothes, so he was probably just being an asshole, and I kept walking, but then I felt a breeze on my butt, a breeze that was just a little too cold. He was right. Blonde Boy could see my underwear and so could all of Sixth Street. I realized that when I put my backpack on at school (about twenty minutes before), my dress had gotten caught and up it went, and everyone could see my old beige underwear, those big old granny underwear that I used to wear because my mom didn't let me buy thongs even though I was almost in ninth grade (or at least bikini underwear like the other girls in my class), and I thought, Trágame tierra! I wanted to be a worm or a mole or a gopher or any type of insect or vermin that lives underground where no one could see me or my calzones de abuelita.

But my mom doesn't understand this. She never does. I don't get it. I guess it's because we have a lightswitch relationship. Sometimes she's wonderful. Sometimes not so much. When she says, "No comas tanto. You're getting fatter than a pregnant woman," she's not so wonderful. But when she says, "She loves to read. She has a 3.75. Mira, le dieron otro certificado," like she knew it all along (that I'm smart and not as bad as she thought), she's the best. On and off. Like light itself—bright and dark. Mother and daughter. That's us. I wish it were different. I wish she would be more understanding, but that's not who she is, I guess.

The pink sparkly dress draped on her arm is for my senior picture. So I will look pretty. Now I'm going to have to wear it, otherwise it would hurt her feelings. Oh well. Asi es la vida. That's my life at least.

August 25

Senior year starts tomorrow! I am sooo not going to be able to sleep. Even Sebastian (who is having one of the saddest summers ever) is looking forward to it. We couldn't stop talking about school but finally just went to bed.

August 26

It was a crazy first day! Luckily I can drive to school now, and that is awesome—even if I have to bring Beto with me. We agreed that we would switch off on radio stations. Otherwise I would have to listen to him bitch about only listening to "main stream" rock. The one bad thing is that Cindy, Sebastian, and I don't have any classes together. I had to change my schedule around to fit my poetry class. Sebastian is in Calculus while I am in Algebra II...again. I only failed because it was boring the way Mrs. Black taught it, and (because the math gods hate me) I have her again this year. I'm so gonna tear my hair out. Four years in a row with the same math teacher? That has to be illegal. On the plus side, Joshua Moore, the super hot White boy I've had a crush on since freshman year, is in my class! Ahhhhhh! I need to relax. Gabi, get a grip!

September 1

Why is Georgina such a fucking idiot? Why? During first period (which is the poetry class that I signed up for because it seemed like fun but turns out is going to be another English class, and while I love English, two English classes means double the writing and double the reading and double the everything else. I so hope I can survive.), Martin Espada asked me if it was true that Cindy was pregnant.

I was like, "What? Who told you that?"

Martin rolled his eyes, "Who do you think?"

Georgina. He didn't have to say her name. Everyone knew Georgina had the biggest mouth in the world since the first grade when Tomasa Jones peed her pants on the slide during recess and Georgina told everyone (even the custodians).

He nodded and asked again, "So is it true?"

I don't know what possessed me to be rude to one of the nicest boys I have every met (he was probably just trying to let me know that Georgina was talking shit about my best friend), but I said, "So is it true you have a hairy ass?"

Martin's face got all red as he stuttered, "What? I was just—whatever," and turned around.

I wish I hadn't been so mean to Martin. He's really nice. And kind of cute. And it turns out he already writes poetry. Good poetry. None of that "the rat is on the mat" shit. But stuff that has meaning. By lunch time, I had heard it from eight different people, and there were eight different stories. In one of them, both Cindy and I had had sex with German—vomit. In another, Cindy didn't know who the father was. The best one was that Cindy had gotten pregnant from some old guy who is now in prison and blamed poor innocent German. Georgina's wild, clown-faced imagination had not failed us. She also said that we'd been in the pharmacy lots of times, getting tests and condoms. Stupid Georgina—if condoms had been purchased, Cindy wouldn't have been in this mess. But no one questioned her stories with logic, and people stayed away from us like we had herpes or something contagious like that. I heard the word SLUTS! thrown at us a few times, but no one owned up to it.

I was pissed. I almost wondered if I should stay away from Cindy. What if my mom was right? What if Cindy was a bad girl, and she would somehow smear her badness on me? But then I realized how stupid and treasonous that way of thinking was. Cindy and I are homies for life. So the three of us—Sebastian, Cindy and I—ate at our usual table and just ignored the stares.

Sebastian tried to lighten the mood and shared that he had met a boy in his Spanish class who had just moved here from Bolivia. And he was gay. And he was cute. And Sebastian was very excited. That kind of took our mind off of Cindy's situation. That and the chili cheese burrito I was shoving in my face.

September 10

My dad is a drug addict. A meth addict—as in crazy and desperate and never mentally here. But no one in our house ever says those words: drugs, addict or meth. It's like we are forbidden to use them. My mom says, "Tu papa anda mal." As if he just has the flu and a bowl of chicken noodle soup will fix him right up. But he's an addict and has been since I was a little kid. I remember when I was in elementary school, he would ask to borrow money all the time. I think even then I knew what it was going towards, but I gave it to him anyway. What was I supposed to do? He's my dad.

It's embarrassing to see him in public, walking around like a homeless person, looking through garbage cans and hanging out with other people with the same "affliction." Sometimes I'm scared that he won't come home. Scared that we'll get a call saying that his body was found in some park bathroom or on the side of some liquor store. I don't know how to help him or what to do to make things better. I think I'm going to start writing him letters.

Dear Papi,

I write this letter to you knowing that you cannot read it because you are too high. I want to let you know that you make me mad. That I would die for you when you're my dad. That I am tired of waiting for you every night and falling asleep at the door hoping you will come home. That I don't want to see you passed out. That I don't want to make breakfast for your "friends" anymore. That I know the money you take from me some mornings is not for gas. That I hate how you make me feel so small when you talk to me like that. That I hate to see Mom cry. That I hate it when Beto cries because you say you don't love him. I know it's the meth talking and not you. The real you used to take us to the park and take me for rides on your motorcycle. Papi, I want you to come back. I don't want the dad who wanders the streets and sleeps in parking lots. I don't want the dad who grows long beards who gives away everything—even his family for a fix. Papi, I want to know when you are coming home, so I can say I love you, and you will understand what those words really mean.

Papi, I miss you.

Gabi

I really have to get some homework done.

September 15

Curse the day I fell in love or like or whatever with Joshua Moore! I hate him. Hate him! HATE HIM! At first I was totally excited that he was in my Algebra II class. Totally excited. But turns out (surprise, surprise), he doesn't like fat girls. Or at least he doesn't like this fat girl. Of course he didn't say, "Gabi, I don't like you because you're a fat girl," but he did start going out with Sandra and she is the total opposite of me.

When I used to be friends with Sandra, my mom was (and sometimes even now) always comparing me to her. She can't seem to understand why I'm not friends with her anymore. I try to explain, but she just doesn't get it. There are things I can't tell my mom either. I can't tell her how Sandra used to make me feel like shit. Especially around boys. Boys like her skinny hips, big butt, long hair, white teeth, big smile and stylish name-brand clothes. Because price is no object when you're a Sandra.

And it wasn't that I was jealous. Okay, I was a little jealous, but she liked to rub it in my face that we were so different. That she was better. She'd remind me that when you're a Gabi, price always matters. No name brand here, only generic, and that is okay until Sandra tells you that it is not okay. I begged my mom for clothes she couldn't afford, asked for something that didn't belong to me, that didn't belong to a world where we get free food from school at Christmas or where your dad spends his money on street corners or where your mom collects cans to make the rent. I couldn't tell my mom that the girl that she's always comparing me to is the reason for so many of our arguments. If I did, she would say something like, "Well, maybe you'd feel better about yourself if you took more care of yourself like Sandra does." And then I'd go do my hair and makeup, squeeze into a pretty little dress and jump in front of a moving train.

I tried to be like Sandra for a little bit. We went to the mall to a super fancy store and bought a very expensive dress. I had to beg my mom for it for weeks until she finally said yes. I felt a little guilty, but my mom gave in because she wanted me to look good and feel good. A brown dress with little white flowers sewn all over, it was short and sleeveless and very 1960s. It was truly a dress. But each time I wore it, my body was exposed— the little brown dress was too expensive for my cheap little white skin. But Sandra thought it looked good, so I felt good (at least about that). Still, I missed the indoor swap-meet with Cindy. Going through the rows of lycra, bright prints, black and whites with no purpose except to make regular girls feel like name-brand girls. To make Gabis feel like Sandras but at a discounted price.

I came to my senses, and Sandra left us. So it was just Cindy, Sebastian and me. Us tackys always have to stick together.

I tried to act like I didn't care about the whole Joshua situation, but it was hard. I came home today and told my mom what was going on (because she's my mom and can ALWAYS tell when there's something wrong and won't let it go until I tell her) and she offered some words of comfort so my heart wouldn't shatter. She knows heartbreak, she said. She said. "Yo se lo que es estar joven y enamorada." I tried to think of my mom as young and in love, but I couldn't, it was too far of a stretch. Secretly I was glad she tried to protect me. It didn't matter though. My heart shattered into a thousand pieces. Just like when you drop one of those Christmas ornaments made with glass so thin that when it shatters it goes everywhere, and you are still finding pieces in dark corners of your living room for months afterwards. That's exactly how I broke. Nothing more to say except that Cindy and Sebastian showed up at my house a few hours ago, and I had the best banana split of my life.

September 16

Today is Mexican Independence Day. While I know we don't live in Mexico, and I am not technically Mexican, there is still a sense of pride that swells in my chest during this day. Being Mexican-American is tough sometimes. Your allegiance is always questioned. My mom constantly worries that I will be too Americana. This morning we were talking about Cindy, and my mom starting saying crazy things like, "The reason Cindy is pregnant is because she was hanging out con esa gabachilla Diana, her neighbor. Remember? That girl who got pregnant by her dad's friend?" My response was, "Yeah, she did. That guy was super old and took advantage of her. It was totally different." "Yeah, but remember how she was always wearing those short shorts? Offering her goodies to everyone? Parecia una hoochie." I laughed so hard because my mom straight out said, "goodies." And "hoochie." She got all embarrassed and told me to hurry up and go to school. So I did. Love my mom.

The other problem with being me—and my Mexican ancestry—is that people don't believe that I am any kind of Mexican. They always think I'm White, and it bugs the shit out of me. Not because I hate White people, but because I have to go into a history lesson every time someone questions my Mexicanness.

I told Sebastian this once and he was like, "It's not a big deal." It may not be a big deal to him because he is a nice Mexican brown. Or a big deal to Sandra who is perfectly dark-skinned. Her Mexicanness is never questioned. Of course. People never say racist things around them. Sandra and Sebastian carry their culture on their skin like a museum exhibit to ohhhh and ahhhhh at. People look at Sandra's long brown hair, dark brown eyes and skin that doesn't need sun, and they think how exotic, how very perfectly Mexican. Not too much to give discomfort—there is no accent, no rough transition from white to brown. A perfect attempt at assimilation, so her brownness can be excused.

Morena. Bonita. Preciosa. Flaca. Flaquita.

On the other hand, I have the kind of skin that is not allowed in the sun for more than fifteen minutes before turning into an overcooked lobster. Sunburn for sure each time I visit the beach. My skin is there for all the world to see and point at and judge. Güera. Casper. Ghost. Freckle Face. Ugly. Whitey. White girl. Gringa. I've been called all of those names. Skin that doesn't make me Mexican enough. Skin that always makes people say, "You're not what a Mexican's supposed to look like." To which I respond, "Well, what is a Mexican supposed to look like? Am I supposed to be brown and short? Carry a leaf blower on my back? Speak with a thick accent? Say things like 'I no spik ingles?' Should I have dark hair and dark eyes, like my mother and grandmother? "

This skin thing always pisses me off. What I need is a nopal on my forehead to let the world know about my roots. One of those flat cactus plants that my grandpa grew behind his house before he died—nopal en la frente. Yup. That would solve all my problems. It would say, "This light-skinned White-looking young lady is of Mexican descent. Really she is. Yes, she speaks Spanish. And English too. She is a sight to see, folks, a real marvel. (Unless you travel to Mexico where there are lots more like her.)" The nopal would solve those problems.

And besides the whole skin situation to annoy me, there are people going around school in sombreros and mustaches and acting like idiots. Apparently along with being brown, we all have mustaches.

At lunch time there were activities for us to participate in, but we skipped out on them because we had heard they were going to be really lame like a churro-eating contest and a guess-that-Spanish-word and the ever popular Mexican Independence Day game—pin-the-tail-on-the-donkey. After lunch was my poetry class, which is not as bad as I thought. Today we actually began writing poems. Ms. Abernard had us write haikus (a Japanese style of poetry that has 5 syllables in the first line, 7 in the second line, and 5 in the last line). Here is a sad one that I just wrote:

> Joshua Moore is gone
> My heart in seven pieces
> I am not lucky

September 20

Having a father who is addicted to meth is exhausting. It's like you have to walk on eggshells all the time. Have to be worried all the time. Have to be scared all the time. And definitely have to be anxious all the time. People on meth are always looking for and thinking about meth. That's it. There is nothing more important to the meth addict than the next fix. They're always chasing something they will never catch and even though they know this, they will never stop chasing it because they can't. It is really sad. We have been on the sidelines watching my dad chase it since I can remember. His teeth are already gone, his skin is getting gross, plus he looks so much older than he is. Sometimes when he's crashed on the living room floor, I just sit and watch him, pretend he's sleeping instead of passed out. Making sure he doesn't die. My father's addiction has also forced me to learn so many things that most of my classmates don't know.

Things I wish I didn't know. I wish I was ignorant like they are. I wish I could come home and unknow and unsee things. I wonder how that would be, having a father who wasn't an addict?

WORDS I'VE HAD TO LEARN BECAUSE OF MY FATHER

Dopamine
Formication
Meth Mouth
Receptors
Tweaking
Methamphetamine
Neurotransmitter
Intravenous
Chronic
Psychotic
Hepatitis B and C
Xerostomia
Dependence
Hyperactive
Obsessive
Aggressive
Depressed

September 23

Why is my life surrounded by so much fucking drama? Why? I just got my SATs back. Obviously I did well, so that is not the dramatic part. People are still talking about how Cindy is pregnant. Like she is the only pregnant girl in the history of our school. This is obviously not the case, though Santa Maria de Los Rosales High School does have a reputation for the least amount of pregnant girls in our school district—a very strange reputation to have. I mean it's not like the students here don't have sex, because they do, but maybe they all use condoms or something. Anyways, people are still running their mouths about the whole situation. German was trying to be nice to Cindy and was sitting at our table at lunch, which was really, really annoying, and it was obvious that it was making her really uncomfortable, but she never asked him to leave. I warned her that he was an ass and that she shouldn't fall for his stupid lines again, and she was like, "Whatever. You don't know anything about these things. You haven't even kissed a guy yet." Ouch. Even Sebastian told her that that was mean. But Cindy was right. I have never been kissed. Never ever. Unless you count Pancho in kindergarten, which I don't. Because at this point in the game, kindergarten kisses don't count. My lips were pure and untouched, waiting for the right moment, for something to come along and snatch them up. Cindy apologized, but it still stings. Plus, I was right. German was just trying to be smooth, but it didn't work because we caught him making out with Sonia in the school parking lot. I didn't throw it in Cindy's face, but I hope she learned her lesson.

Something else happened today. I don't even want to write it down, but I have to put it away somewhere and hope the dirty feeling goes away. This is the thing about drug addicts: all they can think about is getting high. And the consequences—who they hurt or what they have to sell, steal or give away—don't matter. The addict is an insatiable beast. He or she is no longer the person they were before that first high. After the transformation, the beast is always on the hunt. But he will never find what he is looking for. And even if he tries to transform back into the person he was, because that hunger is never satisfied, the beast never goes away. It is always itching to burst through flesh and sinew, turning everything to shit. My father is that beast. Today we found out that he owes a lot of money. So much money that some nice gentleman came to our house to tell my mom that either he gets his money, or she has to sleep with him. Yup, that was the deal that was made. All the money that my mom has been saving for months to see my sick grandma in Mexico... gone. I refuse to believe that my father would make such a deal. That it's some sort of movie shit that doesn't happen in real life. And therefore couldn't happen in *my* real life. But this is the beast we're talking about. The beast has no morals and, Gabi, you better believe that it is very likely that in a moment of desperation, your father completely lost himself. Time for another letter to my dad.

Dear Papi,

I can't find the words to say this, but I will try. This is bullshit. You have broken my heart again. And again. And again. I can't believe you would make us go through this. I want to believe that you would never make a deal that involves trading your wife for drugs, but then I would be lying to myself. I want you to get help. We all want you to get help. You need help. This is the lowest you have ever been. Please get help. Mom is not a prostitute. She shouldn't have to pay your debts. None of us should. I shouldn't have to worry every night that we'll get a call telling us someone found you in a park, beaten, overdosed or dead. I cannot force you to do anything you don't want to do, but I know you want to get better. I know you are tired of living like this. Papi, I love you. Te quiero con todo mi corazon. Come back, please.

Gabi

September 25

My mom called my tía Bertha, my dad's oldest sister, to come see if she could do something about her brother. I really don't know why she called her. It's not like they get along. She always has something to say about everything. "Gabi, don't eat another taco. You'll never find a boy like that." "Beto, your hair is too long, mijo. From behind, you look like a skinny girl. You should cut it." "Cuñada, why do you still have that Virgen de Guadalupe up? You're not still believing in that superstitious nonsense, are you?" It's a good thing Sebastian moved into his tía Agi's house instead of staying here, otherwise tía Bertha would have had a heart attack—she is totally not down with boy-on-boy action. One of her comments did change things though. Beto took her advice and cut his hair—into a Mohawk. HA! The look on tía Bertha's face was PRICELESS when he walked in the door. My mom wasn't too happy about it either, but at the moment there are bigger fish to fry. Good thing Beto didn't tell Mom that I was the one that cut it or else I would have been in deep shit. But since it's him, no one says anything. Beto is always getting away with stuff like that. Always.

I think he's my mom's favorite. Wait, no, I KNOW he's my mom's favorite. It's probably because he's the youngest and a boy. It really pisses me off. But now that tía Bertha is here, Beto and I have an unspoken truce because at the moment we only have each other. To top it off, tía Bertha is super religious. She's not even Catholic, like my crazy tía Lucha who never went anywhere without a rosary, but some other religion that says that women can't wear pants or lipstick or listen to worldly music (live without The Lumineers? I don't think so, sorry God). I couldn't do it.

But my tía Bertha wants to save us all (especially my dad). Calls herself a healer (we call her crazy), a salvationist, (says) she speaks in tongues but mostly those tongues just criticize our wicked Catholic ways, our worshipping idols like la Virgen and los santos. She likens us to pagans but—bless her heart—she never gives up on us. She says that with one touch of her hand anyone is cured! Cured! She says she has seen the holy ghost! That she has been touched by God! Given the gift of sanación! And we do not argue with God! Or question her authority. But I heard rumors. Family stories. The "truths" behind the myth. And I don't know how a bruja, a witch, like her can save our souls.

Last year when we went to Mexico for the summer, my tía Mari told us a story and it went something like this:

She said my tía Bertha resurrected her dead cat, El Negro, when she was seventeen. My tía Mari claims she saw Bertha's head go completely around when she was making tortillas, and then she heard a big THUD y ahí estaba on the floor, foaming at the mouth and her head gone backwards. The priest (I guess someone had called a priest), as was expected, was scared and ran out. Days later my grandmother, convinced it was a seizure, tried to put all the rumors to rest. "No era el Diablo. It was a seizure." It was her daughter. What could anyone expect? After that little incident, they say, tía Bertha bought books on hypnotism, hid family portraits in potted plants, buried and resurrected more dead cats (and maybe even a dog!), tied el lazo de matrimonio de mis abuelitos with black ribbon and buried it in the old outdoor kitchen—the one with the black walls like shiny shoe polish from the smoke that came from the wooden stove. When they found my grandparents marriage lasso tied with a black ribbon (I guess it was a sort of spell), it was the last straw.

The pueblo got wind of Bertha the Demon Possessed Wonder and her wicked doings. (This is where the story gets kind of sad.) When she would walk in the street, she was sprinkled with holy water. People crossed themselves and took their children to the other side of the road and instructed them not to look at her. No one but her family would speak with her. She was twenty-three and turning old maid (in her time). Men were afraid. The fear of being coerced by means of brujeria into marriage stopped them from talking to my poor old tía Bertha. Tía Mari says she became bitter and less social. She spent evenings in a church burning candles for the Virgen, putting that saint of desperate lovers—according to Mexican superstition—San Antonio de Padua on his head, and, eventually, resorting to married men. Tía Bertha reached a low point. But one day everything changed. She met a man from out of state—big lips and long hair. She bewitched him into marriage (so her ex-husband, ex-tío Luis, says). "I didn't know what I was doing!" he claims. But you can't blame stupidity on magic. He's still constantly on the lookout for mysterious powders, sacrificed cats or any indication of brujeria. He never found anything and eventually he left her for a non-witch.

At least that's what I heard.

What is true is that tía Bertha lost her Catholic faith along the way. No one knows how it happened. I asked her about it once and all she said was, "Mija, never trust a seminarian. They don't keep promises. Not even to God." I have thought about what could have happened. Most likely, tía Bertha had a passionate love affair with a handsome seminarian and somehow it went wrong. Whatever it was, from that day on tía Bertha hated Catholics. As for the brujeria, I don't know. Witchcraft is a touchy subject in our house (for various reasons). So far, there has been no evidence to suggest that tía Bertha is a witch. And, except for that birria she turned into maggots one New Year's Eve, I haven't seen anything.

Speaking of birria, I think that's what we're having for dinner. Yay! Spicy little goat, here I come!

September 29

Today was a pretty good day. I think I am finally over Joshua Moore. Sandra can have him all she wants because I now have a huge crush on Eric Ramirez who also happens to be in my Algebra II class. He is soooooo hot! He is light-skinned (not as white as me, but close), has longish brown hair, dresses like a skater and has beautiful brown eyes. He does have one big flaw though—he smokes a little too much weed. I don't know how I feel about smoking. I mean, I know how I feel about it. I think it's just a weed, so whatever. But since my dad is an addict, I don't do any of that stuff. It would kill my mom. Kill her. And I probably wouldn't be able to sit for months. Even if I will be eighteen in six months, she has made it clear that it doesn't matter how old I am, she is still my mother. Besides the whole weed thing, he's pretty awesome. The best part is that Cindy and Sebastian think that he likes me too! Eek!

I don't know though. I don't want to get too excited because I am always afraid that boys will only pretend to like me as a joke. Because, really, who would like the fat girl? Sebastian said I was crazy for thinking that. And Cindy said that was the stupidest thing she's ever heard. She said, "Gabi, you're not fat. Seriously, you're average...okay, maybe a little chubby. I'm not gonna lie and say you're super skinny, but you're not fat!" That's pretty much what they say all the time, but it's hard for me to believe when my own mother is constantly pointing out that I need to lose weight. But maybe they're right. I need to be more positive this year so I wrote a poem about it in my poetry class. We were supposed to write a list poem and so I did it about my goals for this year.

I SWEAR
To make this year better than last
To be positive
To lose weight
To get a kiss
To make out
To get straight A's
To wear a smaller size by the beginning of summer so I can wear that really cute polka dot bikini that I saw at the mall with Cindy who tried it on and of course it fit perfectly but made me look like an overstuffed piñata that had all the candy whacked out and all that was left was colorful tissue paper and cardboard.

I SWEAR
To learn how to put eyeliner on
To be happy in my skin (whatever that means, but it is being said by all those skinny women on TV who don't have much skin to begin with, and so they don't have to worry about how much happiness to fit into their skin,

but us fat girls have so much more skin we have to claw
and scratch happiness from anywhere we can get it so
that we can stuff it into our skin)

I SWEAR
To read more
To write a lot of poems
To not be mad at Sandra anymore

I SWEAR
To not make promises that I can't keep.

I hope Ms. Abernard doesn't get mad because I wrote "make out" and
"get a kiss." And I hope she doesn't make us read them out loud or put
them up on the wall. That would suck big hairy toes.

October 3

Cindy and I went to the mall today after school. Sebastian couldn't go
because he went on a date with Pedro, the cute Bolivian boy from his
Spanish class. I am both happy and worried about that situation. What if
they hold hands and people harass them? What if they get beat up? Why do
I have to worry about these things just because they're two boys? I hope
they're careful. Not that I'm a date expert, but I have been on a couple.

My first date was to the skating rink with a guy named José. (An incident I wish to forget.) Ugh. I hate José. In any case, I hope their date went okay.

Well, anyway Cindy and I went to the mall to pick out some matching shirts to take pictures in. It was a little awkward. I guess I didn't realize how much weight Cindy'd gained. I see her everyday so I hadn't noticed the sudden addition of a little pouch. She's almost four months pregnant.

Wow.

Four months pregnant—in her second trimester. That's something I always hear older women say. The words sound too grown up to belong to us. But they do now. I tried to make her laugh because I don't want her to feel sad. I know it's rough at home with her mom. She told us that her dad won't even speak to her yet and that her grandmother told her that maybe it was time to quit school, that she shouldn't pretend to be a good school girl anymore because—obviously—she isn't. Her grandma and my grandma should be friends. They seem to think alike.

Cindy is my kindred spirit. She laughs when I say that. How I love that girl. She never judges me. Or tries to change me. Nope. She loves me just the way I am. Peas in a pod (uña y mugre, my mom says). We laugh and cry together. Have each other's back through good times and bad times—best friends for life.

And now there's a picture we took at the mall this afternoon to prove it.

October 6

Tía Bertha met Sebastian this afternoon. It was both funny and infuriating. If there is one thing my tía Bertha hates more than Catholics, it's gay people. She hates lesbians more than gay men, but she hates gay men too. I don't know why though. Supposedly, she used to be friends with all sorts of gay men back in the day before she was touched by the hand of God. In any case, now she doesn't like them. I had to introduce Sebastian to tía Bertha again. Because even though she's met him like ten times, she never remembers him.

"Hola muchacho! Que guapo! What a handsome friend you have, Gabi! If only he were a little bit older, maybe he'd take me out on a date." And then she winked at him. Eww. Eww. Eww. But she didn't stop there. "Do you have girlfriend, handsome?" Before I could warn Sebastian about tía Bertha, he laughed and said, "Girlfriend? No! But I have a boyfriend."

I heard Beto shout all the way from the living room, "Oh shit! This is gonna be good!" He is such an instigator. Tía Bertha didn't shut up about the sinfulness of two men together until I couldn't take it any longer and said, "What about the sinfulness of sleeping with a married man?"

I should have kept my mouth shut. That cut really deep. We aren't supposed to talk about her current situation. She just looked at me, hard, her eyes glistening. She was hurt, and I felt horrible. Gabi's diarrhea of the mouth strikes again. My brother just shook his head. If my mom hadn't been at work, I would have been in deep shit. I don't get it though—why do I feel so guilty about saying that to her, but she doesn't feel a little bit sorry about blaming Sebastian for the fall of Sodom and Gomorra, the dissipation of morality in society, and the coming of the anti-Christ?

Later...

Because Sebastian is gay, he is allowed to spend the night since there is no fear that we will have sex and make babies. I finally got to ask him about Pedro. He revealed that Pedro is a really good kisser, has a big "package" (though Sebastian used another word which I feel uncomfortable even writing) and knows a lot of poetry in the mother tongue which he recites to Sebastian (how romantic is that!). He speaks Spanish with a sexy Bolivian accent and is learning a lot of English but is really embarrassed to speak it out loud because of his sexy accent. Sebastian also says his mom is back on speaking terms with him, but his dad is still really angry and doesn't want to see him. He also says that his tía Agi's house is cool and she seems to be loving and accepting. Though she did tell him she doesn't want to see any cochinadas in her house. Which translates to: no sex. Why is every mom's concern about sex? There are more important things in life like school, careers, poetry, books, ice cream or learning how to make the perfect chocolate cake. It's so damn frustrating.

We have to go to sleep because it's like 3 a.m. and we're supposed to meet Cindy early tomorrow for breakfast. And we will go to sleep just as soon as Sebastian is done chatting with Pedro. He was right—he does have a sexy Bolivian accent.

October 12

Okay. Wow. So I realized why moms are so worried about sex: it's everywhere. Like just around the corner. Ahhhhhhh! I can't believe it finally happened. I was in Algebra II and asked Mrs. Black if I could go to the restroom. Of course she let me go (sometimes I think seeing me in her class every day for the last four years may be as unpleasant for her as it has been for me). I didn't really have to go, but I was so bored and needed to get out for fifteen or twenty minutes before I lost my mind from doing one more quadratic equation. I was getting a Dr. Pepper (to go with the Hot Cheetos I was munching on) from the downstairs vending machines, the ones near the science rooms, when I heard some steps coming down the stairs. I looked up and who should it be but Mr. Hot Stuff himself: Eric!

I tried to scarf down the spicy cheese curls and give my Cheeto fingers a quick wipe inside my pockets. In an instant, all I knew was that this was the moment I had been waiting for. For him. For Eric, who makes me stuck for words. Makes me forget about Joshua Moore (who had currently been moved to the front of the class for being an ass—surprise, surprise). He came up to me, and we joked and flirted and talked. I hoped he might see past the waistline and see me—how funny I can be and how cute I giggle and how good I am in language arts. Maybe I just imagined it. Maybe he was just being nice to the fat girl. All those things were rushing through my mind. Until it finally happened—

THE KISSING THING.

Well, kind of. At first, we talked and joked and flirted and talked some more and then...HE TOUCHED ME. Touched me gently on the waist. We were so close, I could smell the peppermint gum he was chewing.

"You know," he said, "I've never kissed anyone." (This could or could not have been a line, but I didn't care and went with it.)

"You know," I said, "I have never kissed anyone either." (That was so lame. I can't believe I said it. Major facepalm.)

"Oh," he said. And I tried to breathe because this was one of those moments where he was making me stuck for words.

"Yeah," I said (like a dumb-ass). But then—and this is what made me believe that I wasn't as big a dumb-ass as I had originally imagined—

his hands on my waist, my back on the wall, my insides on fire, ALL my skin vibrating, lips set—I could almost taste peppermint...suddenly we heard, "What are you two doing?" and saw Mr. Paul's big bald head sticking out of his biology classroom door. "Get back to class before I call security."

I was both embarrassed and devastated—I was going to have to see Mr. Paul later, and he never lets anything go so he'd probably bring it up. We ran upstairs and just as we got to the last step, I turned and kissed him before I could even stop myself.

He was very shocked. Almost as shocked as I was. I had done something I had been thinking about doing, but knew I shouldn't. Things were out of order—I was supposed to wait for him. More embarrassment.

"Wow. I didn't know you had it in you. I guess there's more than meets the eye." That's what he said. Stupid cliché but readily accepted.

I guess there is more to this fat girl than even this fat girl ever knew.

I called Cindy when I got home and told her that something happened, but I couldn't tell her over the phone because my mom might be on the other line. I hate when she does that. I don't know why she doesn't trust me. Then Cindy asked me why I was being old fashioned and using a landline. "I dropped my phone in the toilet," I said. "And my mom said that she wasn't buying me another one. So I guess it's back to the Stone

Age. Pretty soon I'll be writing you letters by candlelight." She laughed, and I told her I'd pick her up tomorrow and then I called Sebastian and told him the same thing.

I really don't get why my mom doesn't trust me and has to listen to my phone conversations or why she doesn't think I'm responsible. I get good grades and try to help around the house, and I don't get in trouble at school. Which is more than I can say for Beto who is currently failing P.E. How do you fail P.E.? I don't know, but apparently my brother does. Yet I am labeled the irresponsible and lazy one.

When I asked my mom what I do that makes me lazy and irresponsible, she said, "I started working when I was five. En el campo. In the fields! Camotes. Beans. Ejotes. Strawberries. Tomatoes and even cacahuates. Stooped over digging in dirt looking for peanuts, picking each green bean, each tomato. Backs hunched over as far as the eye could see so if you looked down the rows all you would see were legs without torsos. We started at the crack of dawn, apenas salía el sol, and there we were with sacks on our backs—stooping, picking, filling, stooping, picking, filling. We'd go home with cracked hands and black nails. Then at seven we would go to mass, tired. But a pinch from your grandma would wake us up. Then to school and then back to the fields. And you can't even throw out the trash?" There was nothing I could say after she said that. After that speech, I actually felt lazy and irresponsible. And a little ashamed of being such a whiner.

October 13

I dropped Beto off at school and told him he better not tell Mom about me ditching first period or else I'd tell her about the girl going out of his window the night before. Then me, Sebastian and Cindy went to Starbucks so we could have some time to speak privately. I couldn't wait to tell them about what had happened. At first it didn't go as planned.

"Wait. *You* kissed him?" asked Cindy.

"Yes!" I said, super excited.

But then she went on and on about how that made me seem desperate and easy and blah blah blah. I wanted to say, "Let's not talk about desperate and easy," but that would have made her cry, and I would have felt like shit afterwards.

Sebastian, however, thought it was pretty brave of me to go after what I wanted. He said that that's what love is all about, not being afraid. Though secretly I know he's afraid. There was a boy from our rival school, JFK High, who had recently gotten the shit kicked out of him because he had been seen holding hands with his boyfriend last week at the mall. The two boys were arrested but released right away. What is this? 1955? But I didn't bring that up either.

"Well, it's not like I planned it. It just happened. It was spur of the moment." I felt like I had to defend myself. "And where is it written that girls have to wait for boys to kiss them?"

None of us knew how to answer that question because it wasn't really written anywhere, but we know it's part of the unspoken set of girl/boy rules.

Cindy said, "Well, I don't know if it was brave or stupid, but I'm glad you had your first kiss." I could tell that she was just trying to cover for what she had said earlier but, since she was my best friend, I forgave her.

I didn't see Eric until our first break. He said, "Where were you this morning? I was looking everywhere for you." I told him that we had been a little late for school. "Oh. Well, I'm glad I found you."

"Por cua?" I asked.

"Ummm...we...like...I know you know now that I like you." At this point, we both got super duper red, and I made some sort of affirmative noise, but no real words would come out of my mouth.

"Weeeellll...I wanted to know...if you...wanted...ummmm...to be... my...you know...girlfriend?"

"What?"

That's how smooth my response was: "What?" I can't believe that was the first word to come out of my mouth. But I couldn't explain to him that I couldn't believe that he, Eric Ramirez—closet history nerd, watcher of stupid television singing competitions, smoker of marijuana, runner of marathons and super hot guy—would actually like me, Gabriela Hernandez— irresponsible daughter, bad girl in the making (according to my mother), semi-decent to possibly good writer, watcher of marathon runners, eater of carne asada tacos (even on Good Friday), and kinda fat girl.

He looked a little surprised—again. He looked uber-embarrassed and said something like, "Oh...I thought..."

I had to interrupt him. "No! I mean, yes! I do want to be your girlfriend. I was just...I don't know...but yes. Affirmative. I will be your girlfriend." And, for some reason, I felt that I had to say that last part in a robot voice. "Sorry, I get nervous and do robot voices."

I lied! I lied about my robot voice! I just did it because it felt like the most natural thing to do at that moment, and if I admitted to him that I felt that way, it probably would have been weirder. I have so much to learn about relationships and being a (normal) girlfriend.

The rest of the day was great (except for Algebra II of course). I have a boyfriend for the first time ever and all of Santa Maria High School knows it. I am happy. Good night.

October 20

Since it's getting close to Halloween, Ms. Abernard assigned us to read about horror, death, ghosts and other stuff related to Halloween—but not really, because if she said it was about Halloween, she could get in trouble. Which is totally stupid. On the plus side, the poems we have been reading are really good. We read "The Raven," by Edgar Allen Poe, which we read last year but is still good this year, and we have been reading poems by Sylvia Plath. Sylvia Plath is very dark and always talking about death and suicide. I love it. My favorite poem so far is, "Lady Lazarus." It's about her trying to kill herself three times and coming back to life just like Lazarus in the Bible—each time another miracle. Except unlike Lazarus, Sylvia doesn't seem to be happy about her return.

Before Ms. Abernard assigned it, I knew what was coming. We have to write a poem about one of the themes we have been reading about. We have already been writing short poems and free writes. Of course Martin already wrote an entire poem about ghosts and death that was brilliant. I think I am going to write about my grandfather who passed away. I miss my abuelito so much. I think about him every day. I can't believe it has already been a year since he died. Tonight when I get home, I will get crackalackin on it.

This is my favorite part of "Lady Lazarus" by Sylvia Plath because she sounds so ballsy—she tells God and Satan to beware! What the hell! *Ugh*. So good.

> Herr God, Herr Lucifer
> Beware
> Beware.

Later that night...

My dad—who had only this morning been passed out on the living room floor—announced that he was going to sober up. He took us all into the living room and had a meeting and told us he was sorry and that he's tired of living to get high, and he wants to be a better husband, father and brother. Tía Bertha swore that his decision was due to her healing powers. "I knew it! Just last night, I felt the hot tongues of the Holy Spirit tickling my ears and then a sudden rush of fire like waves overcame my entire body! This morning I woke up and knew that I had the power to change you, little brother." We all just rolled our eyes but didn't say anything to her. Though I am incredibly happy with my dad's decision, I am also not getting my hopes up—this is not the first time he's tried to quit. But I didn't say anything to discourage him. We all (well, not Beto really) show our support. This time though it feels different. It feels final. So I am going to write him another letter.

Dear Papi,

I am so excited that you have decided to get sober! You have tried this before, but this time I know things will be different. I can feel it. Not in the way that tía Bertha claims to feel things, but deep inside. Things will be hard for a while, and you will probably suffer, but I think it will all be worth it. Life will definitely not be like it used to be. I don't remember a time when you weren't an addict, but Mami does and she says you were an awesome man. I know that when you're not using, you're an amazing person. You're funny and caring and a good person. I can't wait to see you like that all the time. It will be a big change for all of us. But a good change. Maybe when you're clean, you can have a better relationship with Beto. He loves you so much even though you always push him away. Why do you push him away? Is it because he's like you? Stubborn, good hearted, prideful, sensitive and quiet? Maybe. Whatever the reasons, I know things will be different once you're clean. Father and son will get along better and we can grow as a family.

I love you, Papi.

Gabi

Maybe when he's clean I can read him that one.

October 21

Family is one of those things you can't escape and mine is no different. Apparently getting sober didn't mean going to rehab. Why would I think that that is what it meant? Oh, Gabi, you're so funny. No, Dad said he could go cold turkey. Again. That he could stop whenever he wanted to. Again. He has tried this method once, twice, and now he's going for the third time. The hallucinating will start soon. Then he will begin killing demons (inside and out), screaming in pain. The spiders will arrive after that. The bugs under his skin that make him scratch and bleed. It's horrible. I only know what's coming because the first time, when I was twelve, my mom told us what would happen so we wouldn't be scared. I think it was really so she wouldn't be scared. It hasn't really helped. Beto and I slept in the same bed for weeks. I'm not a little kid anymore though, and I know my dad isn't/will never be himself again. He'll always be a man struggling with an addiction and every day will be a battle for him. Like I said, the beast never goes away. And it's calling all the shots. Sometimes it just wants you to think your dad is getting sober and will be the man he wants to be. But the whole time, it's in control.

School didn't really matter today. I told Cindy and Sebastian what was going on, and they tried to be understanding. I really don't feel like I can tell Eric because even though we're going out, I'm not sure I can trust him with something like that. The only two people who know about my dad's "problem" are Cindy and Sebastian and only because of that time we saw him at the park. Talk about being mortified.

Eric was upset because I wouldn't tell him what was wrong, but I said it was girl stuff, and he backed off. He seemed somewhat afraid to touch me after that. I told him it wasn't contagious. He got really uncomfortable so I went to the library to write my grandpa poem, but I couldn't figure anything out. To top it off, I have to start writing the college essays that I should have started writing a month ago. Ms. Rodriguez, my counselor, says we should be on our second or third drafts because they are due at the end of November. Since I want to apply to six different universities, I have a shit-load to write. AHHHHHHHH! I think I should just go to sleep. Maybe I'll be sick tomorrow and not go to school. No, my dad will be home. School will probably be less crazy.

October 26

I don't know how I feel about having a boyfriend now that I have one. I mean, I know how I feel about the kissing and holding hands: I totally love it! But the whole following me around and having to spend every freaking lunch together has me a bit smothered. And to top it off, he told me he loved me! Loved. Me. I didn't know what to say so I acted like there was a bee in my shirt. I didn't want to say "I love you" back because I don't love him, and it would be a lie, and I hate lying. So I wrote a letter to him (that I probably won't send) expressing how I feel about our current situation.

Dear Eric,

I enjoyed the moments we spent together out in the hallway. And by the gym. And in your car. And by the photography classroom. Your breath smelled divine. I like how you remembered to chew some gum before getting really close to me. I obviously forgot as you could smell by the aroma of Hot Cheetos emanating from my soft luscious lips that one time last week. Anyway, I want to tell you how much I like you. I don't think I would, or should, use the word love because that is reserved for special occasions. Not to say that you are not special, just not that special—yet. When I see you, I want to run to you and hug you and throw you up against a wall and feel the wetness of your lips. I want to stroke your hair and hold your hand and walk with you at lunch time and have people say, "Is he really going out with her?" *Maybe that fat girl ain't so bad after all,* they think. I don't want to hurt your feelings, but I don't want to lie to you either. I believe in honesty. Don't you?

Yours fondly,

Gabi H.

I don't think I could bring myself to send it. I don't know how he would take it. I'm going to talk to Cindy about this tomorrow and see what she thinks I should do. Or maybe not. She's been feeling pretty emotional lately, and I'm not in the mood for the Wrath of the Pregnant Girl. I didn't realize having a boyfriend would be so much trouble. I don't want to think about this today. I will think about it in the morning. I guess I might as well finish up my grandpa poem since the first draft is due tomorrow.

October 28

Sebastian is in soooooo much trouble. I feel really bad for him. He wasn't at school yesterday, and today we found out why. The situation is something like this at the moment:

Sebastian has been saying that if his parents don't accept him, it doesn't matter because he doesn't need them. I have been telling him that is ridiculous. They need each other—they're blood. Family. Familia. And while familia is the glue that keeps us crazy, it is also the glue that makes us who we are. So since his parents kicked him out, he has been living with his tía Agi and everything was going well until two nights ago when she caught him con las manos en la masa (to put it mildly) with Sexy-Bolivian-Accent Pedro, who has been whispering poetry and other things to Sebastián in his beautifully spoken Spanish, which, as we know, is the language of romance. So, I guess he was speaking a whole lot of Spanish by the time tía Agi came back home—earlier than expected—from her weekly poker night. And after pants were put back on (Sebastián claims that nothing was going to happen, which sounds really stupid. I mean, why would you take your pants off if nothing was going to happen? I'm a virgin and even I know that much), he tried to talk to his aunt. He told her that they are in love. But tía Agi felt sick and said things like "¡Cochinos! ¡Que asco! You should be ashamed of yourselves!" And they were. She sent Sebastián to a psychologist to talk him out of being gay (I guess she's not as understanding as we thought). And yesterday she sent for a priest who threatened him with God—of course, because everyone knows that the mission that God has left for his worshippers is to hate people and damn them to hell. Finally, she forbade pink shirts, satchels and guy friends who would tempt him with their sinful penises. He is only allowed to talk to me and Cindy because maybe we could make him straight. Maybe she hoped we'd show him our mighty vaginas and fuck the gay out of him. Maybe she figures Cindy is a good candidate for sleeping around. Adults make stupid assumptions. But I don't think tía Agi understands that it doesn't work like that. That being straight is not a choice, or that being gay is not a choice.

So that's why Sebastián is currently sleeping over at my house on a school night. Tía Agi is probably at home praying that we're having sex right now. She'd be so disappointed if she knew that all we are doing is sitting around talking about boys and pretending to do homework.

October 30

Today was the big day in poetry class. Ms. Abernard had us read our poems IN FRONT OF EVERYONE. Martin did great. His poem had some words in Spanish and so does mine. We have been practicing using two languages in writing since after we read some poems by two superpoets: Michele Serros (who is still alive AND from California!) and Sandra Cisneros (she's still alive too, but not from California). Before we read their poetry, I didn't even know you could use two languages in a poem. I thought they either had to be in English or Spanish. Turns out I was wrong. Michele Serros has a really funny poem (poems can be funny too! Who would have known?) titled "Dead Pig's Revenge." It's about a girl who loves eating chicharrones and ends up choking on one. Oh my God, I could relate to loving food like that. That's probably why I love the poem so much.

Martin wrote a poem about La Llorona that somehow had something to do with his mother and grandmother and great-grandmother. I had to read my poem after him and was really nervous because everyone loved his poem, and I was afraid that people would laugh at mine. But I was wrong—they loved it. It was probably because Martin helped me figure out how to do line breaks and where to start a new stanza and all of that stuff that I hadn't been paying close attention to. Ms. Abernard said my poem was really good and suggested that I put it in the journal our class is starting, *Black Cloud*.

Here is the poem I wrote:

WHEN YOUR GRANDFATHER DIES

When your grandfather dies,
ask yourself
if God exists,
because I don't think it's possible,

not when you see that old man
still
in a bed,
closed eyes,
head on chest,
not asleep,
not in his home,
but in a hospital where
he didn't want to be.

And when you get to his funeral,
don't look in the casket
no matter how much you think you want to,
don't,
because that's not your abuelito

who shook trees
and made the limes rain.

That's not abuelito who bought you
dulces de coco raspados and paletas.

That's not him in that box
with the little flowers painted on the outside
and the embroidered cross on the inside
for a safe journey.

That's not your abuelito who held you.
That's not your abuelito who was ninety years old
and still mowed his own lawn,
kept nopales in his backyard
and fed a dog
named Palomo.

That's not him at all.

Your abuelito would have worn a hat
to cover his bald head.
And he had a broken nail with dirt underneath
from pulling out weeds all morning long.
And he had more wrinkles.
He smelled like Zest and Old Spice,
and took naps in the sun.
And he, he awoke when you called him.

In that box
is just an old man who looks like him,

who is going in a hole in the ground (forever),
who will not be there when you get married,
who will not meet your children,
who will go under the earth and rocks and grass,
no matter what you say or how much you scream or cry.

When you look at his pictures,
you will ask for forgiveness,
and when you stand on the ledge of that bridge ready to jump,
you won't because he would be disappointed.

Songs will remind you of him,
especially the one that goes,
"Me caí de la nube que andaba.
Como a veinte mil metros del altura."
Because he sang that song to you
every time you said,
"Abuelito, cántame la canción."
And he knew what song you were talking about
because he knew you like nobody did.

You will walk to his grave
next to your grandmother's
and ask him
if there is a god,
and he will not answer because he is dead.
But because you still know what he's thinking,
you will know the answer.

I started working on a second part to that poem about my grandmother dying. Just for fun. Martin told me he liked the poem. I think I might have a crush on him. Oh my God! I just realized that. I can't have a crush on him though because I'm going out with Eric. Or can I? Would that be wrong? Does that make me a slut? Does that make me a wicked city woman? Probably. I need to stop watching those "I Love Lucy" reruns. I am going to have a grilled cheese sandwich and think about this precarious situation.

Later...

I just got off the phone with Eric. I guess he told his family all about me and they all want to meet me, especially his abuelita. His abuelita? Precarious is definitely the word of the day.

October 31

Halloween was stupid. As usual.

November 4

This month's poetry assignment is about being thankful. So cliché, Ms. Abernard, so cliché. I think the poem about my grandmother dying may fit in this category, so I am just going to keep on working on it and turn that in. Cindy is looking totally pregnant now. We went shopping yesterday, and she actually had to get maternity clothes. Maternity clothes have this weird wide elastic waistband. They are hideous. I was glad we got to go together though, just me and her. I love Sebastian, but sometimes I just want some girl time with Cindy. So when we got back to my house and during our pepperoni pizza delight, I asked her something I had been meaning to ask her for a while and had been too embarrassed to do. I asked her what it felt like to have sex. Our conversation went something like this:

ME: Hey, Cindy?

CINDY: ¿Que pasa, calabaza?

ME: I want to ask you something very personal. But since you're my best friend, I thought I could ask you.

(She looked at me very suspicious.)

CINDY: Okaaaay...you're not going to try to get me to walk you through using a tampon again, are you? Because that didn't go over so well last time.

ME: No! Besides, I'll get it. Eventually. What I wanted to know was, what did it feel like?

CINDY: What did what feel like?

ME: (Feeling my face turning super red but not about to give up on finding out this useful information) Sex. It.

CINDY: It? You mean German's thing? (Now she turned red.)

ME: Well, yeah.

CINDY: Well, you know what it feels like. You've felt one before.

(I knew what she was talking about, but it was a totally different situation.)

ME: Are you talking about the time at that quinceañera?

We burst out laughing. It was like two years ago, before I started keeping a diary. But I will record it anyway because I never want to forget this.

We were both wearing white pants, black blouse, black heels, red lipstick, black liner and thick mascara. It was a quinceñera for some girl we didn't know. Her dream day was filled with strangers who were friends of friends that her mom's cousin and dad's uncle's nephew's sister-in-law invited from work. Cindy's mom drove us. We got a table close to the dance floor because that's why we were there—to get our groove on. As soon as we got situated, Cindy's mom put the centerpiece—fake fuchsia flowers around a vase with a white candle in it, embraced by a glittery porcelain white doll (never mind that the real quinceañera was the color of tamarindo) and big Mis XV Años on the doll's dress—inside her purse. Typical Cindy's mom behavior. Cindy looked hot. And I guess I didn't look that bad because right away this guy asked me to dance. He too was wearing tight white pants, plus sombrero de lado (I used to think that wearing your hat to the side like that was sexy but not anymore). Buttons opened down his chest on his silk Virgen de Guadalupe dress shirt, exposing a fat gold chain that wrapped his neck, tangled in chest hair and dangling a big fat cross. Our lord and savior staring straight up at me as we danced. As he squeezed me tighter, sweat began to drip down homeboy's chest and then...I felt it. I remember thinking ewww ewww ewww! For the first time in my life, on my hip, a man's manhood. It was touching me. Dios mio. OMG. I did the first thing that came to mind to save me from further exposure to the male anatomy which seemed to be where this guy was headed—I said, "Mi amiga, Cindy, tiene muchas ganas de bailar contigo. Seriously, my friend Cindy loves to dance, ask her." Cindy was pissed. Turned out it was her first time with it too.

ME: Okay so that was not what I was talking about. You know that. Did it hurt?

(Cindy got this weird look on her face, like she didn't want to talk about it.)

CINDY: (She sighed and looked away from me.) No, it didn't feel good at all. For me at least. I mean, it hurt and wasn't what I expected it would be like. I thought it would feel good, but it was mostly uncomfortable, after the pain was gone. There was a little blood on my underwear when I got home. It was just...it was so...I don't know. It was definitely not how I imagined I would give it up. I mean we did it in the back of German's mom's car. And you know how dirty she is. There was a mess in there. I think there was a Cheerio in my butt at one point.

We couldn't stop laughing after she said the Cheerio in her butt. We finished our pizza, and then Cindy went home to start work on college applications (I am so happy that she's sticking to that part of our plan at least). That was like thirty minutes ago. I guess I should get working on those applications too. I already finished my first personal statement. I figure I can tweak it for each one. They all ask for pretty much the same thing. Okay, now I am seriously going to get started on these applications.

November 6

I can't believe I got a "C" on my Algebra II test. I totally thought I was going to fail it. That means that my mom was right. I just need to study more. I won't tell her that though, otherwise she would probably rub it in my face. I think Eric is growing on me a little more now. But I still can't stop thinking about Martin either. I have written Eric a few more letters (that I obviously won't send because as a girl I cannot be too forward, at least that is what my mom says—"No seas ofrecida. You seem desperate.")

Querido Eric,

Tus labios se sentían tan suaves. Gracias por todo.

G.

Dear Eric,

What's up? How have you been since last we conversed? I have been ok. Thinking about you and our kisses.

Me.

Eric,

I am getting really tired of writing letters and not sending them to you. What I really want to say is that I really like kissing you. But maybe I just like kissing. I am very confused because though I like you, I also like Martin. And maybe even Joshua still. I know what you are thinking. Well, not really because you are not reading these letters. But in any case, you would probably think, *What a slut!* And I don't know if I would agree with you because I simply cannot help the way I feel. Can you help the way you feel? If so, good for you but I kind of like the way I feel. Though I would never admit it because you would say something like, "I thought fat girls were different." And I would say, "Fat girls are different."

Gabi

Whoa, Gabi, where did that last letter come from? Thank God, I ain't sending them. I wonder what Martin is doing. He looked so cute with his new red Converse on today. My mom's knocking on the door so I have to go hide these Cheez-its and open the door.

Later...

My mom found the Cheez-its. I don't get it. It's not like she's a supermodel. Why does she always have to be telling me to lose weight? "Es por tu bien! You need to be healthy. Do you want diabetes? Look at your grandma. She has diabetes and has to use insulin and she may even have to go through dialysis. Do you want dialysis?" Obviously not. Who would want dialysis? But I can't say that to her because otherwise I'll get the old one-two to the face. Well, she's always threatening to hit me but never does. I mean she has hit me a few times. The last time she tried to, I ran from her and her furry pink chancla to my room, wrapped myself in my blankets, and wiggled around screaming and crying like a lunatic. My mom felt really bad. And then I did too. But I really didn't want to get hit. In any case she found and confiscated my delicious cheesy treats, made me vacuum under the bed because she swears mice will invade, and said I have to start working out again. Yeah, that'll happen. I have too much shit to do this month. Working out will have to wait until

December after all college applications are sent out and all that is left is to wait for rejections.

Right now though, I am going to try not to think about where my dad is going. He decided that living sober was not the path for him. I can hear him taking his bike out of the garage. Sigh. Yup, there's the fence and there goes my dad. I'll say a Padre Nuestro and a Hail Mary for him tonight. And maybe tomorrow, I'll write a poem about it.

November 10

I don't know whether to laugh or cry right now. I guess laughing would be bad because this is a serious situation. My mom got a call as soon as I got home from school that Beto had been arrested. ARRESTED. Ha! Okay, not really funny, but it kind of is. She's always saying what a great kid he is and how wonderful and how blah blah blah. He's her favorite. But today my little darling baby brother got arrested. Him and his friend Miguel Juarez to be exact. They got caught tagging up the side of a freeway...during the day...during school hours. Really? But this is the kicker: Beto gets arrested, and my mom blames me. She yells at me the whole time on our way to pick him up and says, "Is this what you teach him? ¿Ese es el ejemplo que le das?" I want to scream, *I am not his mother! You are!* But I cannot remind her of this, or it is to the chancla I go, no matter how old I am. I cannot remind her that she has let him slide. She has expected less of him, and he has realized this. I cannot remind her that our father gave up, but that she doesn't have to. I am pissed off. Very pissed off. And this is the part that isn't so funny. Her perfect son, the little one that breaks no plates, the quiet one, got caught tagging and destroying public property—and she knows she's responsible. He's got talent, and I hope he sees it one day. But right now I can hear the disappointment in the other room—my mom's voice cracking and the silence from the other side. She's made him throw out everything he's kept hidden in the closet that no one has bothered to look in until now: spray cans, markers, rollers, masks. And then I hear, "What the hell do you want with a fire extinguisher?!" And I wonder the same thing. I have failed as a sister. This I know because my mother told me so, and my brother is proof.

But I can't think about it too much right now. Too long of a day. Gonna work on second drafts, work on economics project, work on my grandma poem and then I'll check in on my brother. My mom will have left him alone by then.

Later...

I just talked to my brother. He is really upset about the whole situation and says he doesn't know why anyone cares. No one loves him, he said. "What?" I said, "You're crazy. I love you." He says I don't show it very much since I am always out with my friends and stuff. Which is true, I am. I mean not all the time because I can't go out all the time, but I would much rather be with my friends than hang around this place and listen to my parents argue or watch my dad waste his life and money away. Plus Beto's fifteen, and I'm seventeen. I like school, and he doesn't. He likes to smoke weed, and I don't. He's had like a billion little girlfriends, and all I've had is Eric. He has a whole group of friends he hangs out with, I have Cindy and Sebastian. He can play the guitar, and I can type fast. He is six feet tall, and I'm not. I promised him I would spend more time with him and take him out more. But he really pissed me off because as soon as I said that, he asked if I would take him to buy some new markers and spray paint. Sometimes I wonder if we're even related.

November 15

My mom is pregnant. Can my life get any more complicated? I can tell she's not happy about it because she was really sad when she told us. The baby is going to be eighteen years younger than me and sixteen years younger than Beto, who seemed excited. He said he always wanted a little brother. I said I always wanted a little goat, but that ain't happening. No one thought that was funny. I don't get how my mom got pregnant since she and my dad have a dysfunctional relationship: he's always high, and she's always mad about him being high. And after that guy came by to collect what was owed a few months ago, I don't know how she would let him touch her. But my dad seemed really excited, just like Beto. I don't know why though, it's not like he's such a great father to the kids already out of the womb. It sounds harsh, I know, and I love my dad with all my heart, but what was he thinking?

Cindy and Sebastian tripped out when I told them. They couldn't believe it either. Sebastian wondered if the baby would be okay because my dad uses drugs. I assured him that it only mattered if my mom used drugs. *Is* my mom using drugs? That would be the only logical explanation for this unfortunate situation. I told Eric and he was like, "Congratulations!" He knows very little about my family, otherwise I doubt he would be congratulating me. He has a little baby brother and two older sisters and two loving, seemingly normal parents. I met his abuelita last week, and she was really sweet. She said I was very pretty and commented on how white my skin was.

Never fails. They were also surprised when I spoke Spanish. I swear I should take this show on the road.

A new baby...that means there will be crying and diapers and more messes and more laundry and more money needed. Does that mean I'll have to get a job? Will I still be able to go away to college? My mom is always going on about how good Mexican girls stay home and help their families when they are in need and how that differentiates us from other people. Kind of wishing I was other people right now if that is what is going to determine my Mexicanness at the moment. My mom should have taken her own advice—ojos abiertos, piernas cerradas. If she would've kept her eyes opened and her legs shut, we wouldn't be in this mess. I'll think about that later though. Right now I need to finish typing the final draft of my personal statements. I was surprised at how well they came out. Tomorrow I will put all my application packets together and send them out. Thank God for fee waivers and saved-up birthday money.

Just realized that there are now two pregnant women in my life, and both of them are in very similar situations. I won't tell my mom though because she'd probably be pissed. I have to work on that poem about my grandma. I'm finding out that I really like poetry. It's therapeutic. It's like I can write something painful on paper and part of it (not all of it, obviously) disappears. It goes away somewhere, and the sadness I feel dissolves a little bit. I've always liked poetry, but I didn't realize how powerful it could be. Gotta go to sleep, otherwise I will not be able to do anything tomorrow.

November 16

College applications were sent out. All six of them. Four state schools and two dream schools. In a perfect world, I would be accepted to all of them, and I could just pick and choose, but I have a feeling that those dream schools will just stay dream schools. Especially Berkeley. Berkeley is my number one choice. Berkeley has an awesome English program which is what I want to study. Ms. Abernard suggested I study English and take creative writing classes but then get a Masters in Fine Arts—an MFA—in poetry. I don't know what I would do without her. Besides having a great English department, Berkeley is only a hop-skip-and-a-jump away from San Francisco.

SAN FRANFREAKINGCISCO.

I went there last year with my mom to visit a friend of hers, and it was such an amazing city. When you are there, you feel alive and motivated and inspired. Ms. Abernard said a lot of famous poets have made their home there, and that it has a poet-friendly community. I pray every night for the college gods to admit me into Berkeley.

Cindy, Sebastian and Eric have not sent any of their stuff out yet.

Cindy says she's scared she won't make it. She's thinking about just getting a job at the doctor's office where her mom works as a receptionist. I told her that was a dumb idea, that she wanted to be a doctor, not work for a doctor. And that, since she was going to have a baby, she should try to be a good role model by not giving up on her dreams. She said she would send the applications out (thank God). I hope she didn't just say that so I would shut up. Eric said he might consider going to community college, but that he was hoping to become a famous skate boarder. I laughed out loud and said, "What?" I thought he was kidding, but he was totally serious. I need to do something about this relationship. Sebastian also wants to get into Berkeley...far far away from Santa Maria de los Rosales, CA. It would make sense for him too. I mean Santa Maria is known for smog and overcrowded highways, not for its love and acceptance of gay folk. But still...I love my city with the same force that I love my dad. There's no escaping my roots, and I guess it's better to embrace them than cut them.

Now to finish that poem. One more rewrite of the last stanza of my poem about my grandma and I'll be ready to read it tomorrow.

November 17

Read the poem and got a mixed reaction from the class. Some of the people said they liked it, and some said it was mean. Those that thought it was mean said that I shouldn't talk about my grandma that way because she's dead and that it was disrespectful and blah blah blah. But Martin came to my rescue and said that the poem was supposed to be about giving thanks. And that my poem, although unconventional (he actually said "unconventional"—what is he, like 30?), expressed how thankful I was about my grandma not suffering anymore.

Here's my unconventional poem.

WHEN YOUR GRANDMOTHER FORGETS

When your grandmother forgets,
she will forget all about you
and God.
She will forget how to knit,
how to make tortillas,
or why she exists.

She will wander the streets,
lost in her city.
Her mind will crumble behind her,
and you will scramble,
picking up pieces
that she will reject

because
she does not remember you.

And you will say things like,
"Abuelita, soy yo, Gabi."
And she will try to place you,
but she can only find one memory.

"When you were small,
you were lost for two hours,
we couldn't find you in the park.
You were by the lake looking at ducks,
feeding them bread
that you got from who knows where."

Si, abuela, si me acuerdo.

"I remember, Gabi, when you were small.
You were lost for two hours,
we couldn't find you in the park.
You were by the lake looking at the ducks,
feeding them bread
that you got from who knows where."

"When you were small..."
and that is all that is left.
It will go on
until you go home.
Empty.

And when your abuela dies,
you will feel guilty.
Because...
well, because you are thankful.
Because at least now
she can't forget anymore.

Reading it again makes me see how it could seem a little heartless, but—
in my defense—seeing my grandmother forget who we were and—worst
of all—forget her own son was very painful for everyone, even her. My
dad got so much worse after she died. We didn't see him for one month
straight after that happened. It was the most stressful time in my life. We
all were afraid he had died somewhere and didn't have ID on him, so the
city just cremated him, and we wouldn't ever know what happened. Still,
I would fall asleep by the door waiting for him like when I was a little girl.
When he finally showed up, he was thin and his beard had grown, and he
hadn't showered and smelled bad...I almost didn't want to let him in the
house. But I did. Good Mexican girls never turn away their parents, no
matter how awful they've been. My mother taught me that.

Besides, I love him.

November 20

Eric was such a jerk today. We went to the mall with Cindy and Sebastian. We were looking inside one of the stores, and there was this rainbow-colored tutu thing so Eric thought it would be funny to pull it out and say to Sebastian, "Hey, look, you could wear this to school on Monday and show some pride!" First off, *What?* Secondly, *What an asshole*. I gave him a mean look, and he got all mad, and we had a big fight about him being stupid, and he said, "You know what, fine. I'll just call my mom to pick me up." I think he expected me to be like, "Oh no, don't do that. It's okay, I'm sorry!" But the fool thought wrong because I said, "Super. That's one less trip I have to make." And walked away with Cindy and Sebastian. He looked pissed. But oh well, he shouldn't have acted like that. Sebastian tried to make it seem like it wasn't such a big deal, but I know it had stung. He has been overly sensitive to things like that since his stupid tía Agi has been making him go to the pray-the-gay-away sessions. I think he should stop going, and he says that if he does stop going, he won't have anywhere to live, that his tía said the only way he could stay with her was if he kept going. I wish I could be like, "Oh, just come live with us. No problemo." But the truth is, I don't even want to be at my house so I definitely don't want to put someone else through that misery.

November 24

It's Thanksgiving. Holidays at the Hernandez household can go one of two ways: as planned or disastrous. Thanksgiving last year consisted of going to my tío Beto's house and having a Thanksgiving meal that his crazy wife cooked for us. The whole time I was eating, I was praying because—while it tasted delicious—she could have (and would have possibly) poisoned us. That would be an example of a holiday going as planned.

Christmas, however, rarely goes as planned. Last year we spent Christmas Eve at the hospital because my dad accidentally ran over my foot when he was backing up in the driveway. Was he drunk? Yup. Did we take the keys? Of course not, why would we? This year, Thanksgiving seems to be on track. Tía Bertha is making a ham and mashed potatoes, Mami is making macaroni and cheese, and green beans, and Sebastian (who is spending the night) is bringing tamales that his tía Agi made. Our neighbor Rosemary always sends two pies over: apple and pumpkin. She is a super sweet old lady and an excellent baker. When I was a kid, I used to visit all the time because she let me help her in the kitchen. I still go over at least once a week. She's teaching me how to make pies. That is a dangerous skill to teach this food lover. We've already made coconut cream and apple. Next week is strawberry. *Mmmm*, my favorite. I even wrote a haiku for pies.

Blissful strawberry
I will walk with you all night
Coconut melody dream

Later...

This holiday went as planned. My dad was surprisingly coherent, tía Bertha didn't mind that Sebastian (the bringer of the anti-Christ) was present or that abuelita Gloria took about ten hours saying a prayer (all of which was in Catholic). Mami didn't get angry, Beto didn't instigate and the meal was delicious. It would be awesome if all our holidays were like this, but we could never have such good luck. I ate too much mashed potatoes and too many tamales, and now my stomach feels as though it is going to burst. Just laying here writing is painful. Ugh. But today is one of those days that I have to take one for the team (the team being me, myself and I). I still have to sneak a slice of pumpkin pie and whipped cream before my mom puts it away. Just realized I haven't talked to Eric since the day I left him at the mall. I wonder if we're still dating? Boys are so complicated.

November 28

I had a feeling that our Thanksgiving Day bliss would not last. As soon as I got home today, I knew something was wrong. Usually I drive Beto home, but today my mom picked him up because I had to work on a project for my government class. We're making a mock presidential campaign and we started working on the scripts for commercials today. They are hilarious. But anyway, I got home and Beto was already there, sitting on the front porch and upset. There was a drill, a jigsaw, some screws and some planks of wood leaning against the wall. This had Dad written all over it.

ME: What happened?

BETO: Nothing.

ME: What happened?

BETO: Why doesn't he love me? Why doesn't he care about keeping promises, about how he treats us, about Mom, about you, about me? He doesn't care about anything except getting fucking high! That's all he cares about, getting high. I hate him! He's a fucking asshole!

(By this time he was sobbing and I was trying not to.)

ME: What did he do?

BETO: He said he was going to help me build the ramp in the backyard. We went to the store, got all this stupid shit. On our way back, his stupid friends called him, and he dropped me off with the stuff and left. He said he would be back, but that's another fucking lie! He's been gone four hours! Why doesn't he love me, Gabi? Why?

He picked up the hammer and broke the unbuilt ramp. Smashed the drill. And broke the jigsaw. I couldn't stop him, and part of me didn't want to because he had to let it out. When he was done, I grabbed him and held him. We went to the porch steps, and we sat there. I knew that it wasn't about the stupid ramp. My dad just doesn't keep promises—ever. Not to the people who love him anyway.

When we were kids, he would tell us he would take us bowling on Saturday mornings. Beto and I would get up early, get ready, and wake him up—like he said to do. Instead he would wake up and say, "Otro dia. I have other things to do." He did have other things to do, and we would get dragged along to those things. Things like waiting in cars for him while he did pick ups. Sometimes it would be two hours before he got out. And it didn't matter what time of year it was—summer, winter, spring, fall. We would be in the car during 100 degree weather or during rain or hail or winds or on a beautiful day when other kids would be going to the park with their dads.

Now that we're teenagers, we don't go with him anymore. And he knows better than to ask us. Me especially. He tried that shit a few weeks ago, asking me to take him to his friend Flaco's house. I told him that I wasn't a kid anymore, and if he loved me he would never ask me to do that again. He looked like he felt really bad, but I had to do it.

My baby brother is different. He doesn't say much, but he feels a lot of anger and sadness, and he can't scream it out loud or eat through it like I do. Most of the time he hides it well, but I know it's there underneath, simmering, coming to a slow rolling boil, and one day it will explode. It will spill over, drowning and scalding everything in its path. Today was nothing compared to what I am afraid will happen one day. When my dad is in a drugged stupor, he always lets him know just how much he thinks he's worth. Little Brother cries and asks, "Why don't you love me?" Our father, the beast, answers, "Vete con tu madre, ella si te querré."

And she does, even if she's always scolding us. It seems like my mom is the only one who loves us.

My brother is fifteen. He knows many things. He knows how to make a pipe out of an apple, and he knows how to make beautiful murals on public property. He likes wrestling and biking and skateboarding but doesn't like school because school doesn't understand kids like us. My brother—the brat, the crybaby, the quiet one, the brown one, Mami's s favorite: where will he go? I ask myself that question over and over. Y no se. I don't know where he will go, but I hope wherever it is it's better than here.

November 29

I finally talked to Eric today. He was really pissed that I left him at the mall. I reminded him that he was the one who said he was going to call his mom to pick him up and that I never told him to do that. He said that he had expected me to stop him. What? Why would I do that? Of course I never said that because it would just cause another fight. He said whatever and that he was sorry for insulting Sebastian but that he didn't know blah blah blah. So, I guess we are still dating. I thought I would feel good about it, but I really don't. Maybe it's all the shit going on at home or all the school work I am doing (I still have to write that paper on *Brave New World* and finish reading and responding to five poems for my poetry class, study for the math mid-term *aaaaand* finish filming the commercials for government) or all the drama in Cindy and Sebastian's lives. This is too much. Way too much. I may take Sebastian's offer for tomorrow and ditch with him and Pedro. But I don't know. I've never done something like that. If my mom finds out, she'll kick my ass. Cindy said she would, but that, in her current condition, drugs would affect the baby, and it could come out deformed. Which made me question what deformity would be born from me if I went and smoked weed with them.

November 30

THANK GOD I DIDN'T GO. So, this morning after third period, when Sebastian and Pedro were getting ready to ditch, I told them I couldn't go. That I had a really bad feeling about it, and if I went my mom would literally kill me. One drug addict is enough in our house, thank you. Pedro said you can't get addicted to weed, but if I was chicken, then fine. I said, "Cluck you." They just rolled their eyes and left. I didn't see them after school either, but Sebastian texted Cindy who then called me (I really need to find a way to make money to replace my phone) and told me everything. It turns out that Pedro and Sebastian went to Skyline and almost as soon as they lit up, THE COPS APPEARED! Well, of course Sebastian started crying and saying how he couldn't get arrested because his tía would kick him out because now he would be gay *and* a druggie, and she wouldn't want that in her house and all this and that. The police asked which car was theirs (apparently Sebastian was crying the whole time—he is definitely not cut up to be an outlaw) and, since they had probable cause, they searched it. Pedro, however, had a lot of weed on him. A LOT. Enough to get him arrested. Sebastian didn't know that his little Bolivian with the sexy accent was selling. Finding that out made him more hysterical, and the police thought it was obvious that he had no idea what was going on, and they LET HIM GO! What?! I mean, that's a good thing, but that is some pretty bad police work. I am so freaking happy I didn't go with them. I would have been totally fucked. I wouldn't have been able to see my friends until I was eighty. Sebastian said he learned his lesson, and that he would never smoke weed again in his whole entire life. Unless it was legalized.

Later...

Ms. Abernard is the coolest teacher. Ever. She has us read the usual school board-approved stuff that won't get her into trouble. But since she knows some of us from the poetry club she used to run, she gives us a secret reading list. The reading list is very secret because she could get fired (or something like that) for giving it to us. So she only gives it to people she can trust: Martin, Lindsay, Harold, Jackie and me. This week we were learning about spoken word, and she said that if we were going to learn about spoken word, we needed to learn about the Beats. She gave us a poem to look at and think about, a poem written by Allen Ginsberg titled "Howl." I was in shock that Ms. Abernard could trust us with such poetry. I mean the first lines are, "I saw the best minds of my generation destroyed by madness, starving hysterical naked, / dragging themselves through the negro streets at dawn looking for an angry fix." That's the magic of poetry—some gay Jewish poet wrote about people wasting away around him because of drugs, and I, a straight Mexican-American girl, know how he felt because I am seeing the same waste he witnessed over fifty years ago. Ginsberg is talking about my dad in those first lines. He didn't know it then, but he was.

I was inspired by the poem and by the spoken word poet that Ms. Abernard invited to our class today. Her name is Poppy and her poetry was about being Black and trying to find herself and losing weight and being a woman and...she was awesome! She said that spoken word poetry was different because it was meant to be read out loud as a performance. She also invited the class to participate in an open mic at a coffee shop called The Grind Effect on the other side of Santa Maria. I have driven by that place once or twice on my way to the mall but have never been inside. Poppy's talk made me want to try to write a spoken word poem about my dad. I don't know why, but it seems like the perfect form to talk about him. I started writing like two hours ago, and I think I'm almost done, but I will have to finish tomorrow because I am really tired.

December 1

I wasn't able to sleep last night because I had to finish my poem. And—
because I had to finish my poem—I didn't finish my math homework. Ah!
Algebra II is the only thing stopping me from getting into college. I have
to pass it because otherwise I will not get into any of the schools I applied
to. Need to focus. Today Jessica Smalls, Javier Rubio and I presented our
campaign commercial in government class and everyone thought it was
hiliarious. We filmed it at a park and did some cheesy special effects. At one
point, we dressed Javier up like a baby and had Jessica kiss him. Even Mr.
Reyes laughed at that. I hope we get an A. At lunchtime, I saw Eric (he is
really really starting to annoy me), and we hung out. I don't feel like I have
a lot to talk to him about. It feels like all we do is make out. And, while I
like that, I would love to have someone to talk to about poetry and friends
and family. I still don't feel like I could trust him with my family situation,
and he hates poetry. We are not a match made in heaven, but I still have
feelings for him and want to try and work it out. To top it off, Beto caught
us making out by the gym on his way to P.E. "New shoes," was all he said.
Fuck, I thought. There goes the cell phone money I had been saving up
from cleaning Rosemary's house. So I have to take him to the mall after
school today to buy him some new shoes so he won't tell my mom.

Later...

Just when I thought things couldn't get worse...I went to the mall today with Beto. I stared out the window of the shoe store—people watching. There were couples hand-in-hand across the second-story bridge that connects the Vans store to the food court. I see ice cream cones dripping on the blue mall carpet near the pretzel shop, and then I see familiar blue braces. It's Eric. I hadn't told him I would be coming to the mall today—it was a lucky coincidence. I stepped to the doorway to wave hello and immediately stopped when I saw Sandra. Sandra and Eric kissing. Dripping ice cream all over the floor, making a big mess. My brother sees what I see and puts the shoes back.

"I didn't want them anyway."

We drove back home in silence. I tried not to cry. And was able to wait until I got into my room and shut the door. I pulled some Kit-Kats from my underwear drawer and chewed my heartache away.

ERIC THE HEART BREAKER

Eric who said he loved me
Eric who said forever
Eric who was my first kiss
Eric who always gave me the pepperoni off his pizza
because it is my favorite

Eric who never called me fat
Eric who took me home to meet his abuelita
Eric who never lies

lied to me.

Took my heart
and laughed at it.
Deep fried it
milanesa style
made a torta
and ate it.

No remorse.
None at all.

He's a fucking cannibal.

Now I know why Sylvia Plath had so much to write about. Writing when you're sad is so much easier. And it makes you feel a little better.

December 2

It's a good thing I have a brother who has my back, who is willing to do illegal things to get revenge on behalf of his sister. This morning in the school parking lot, Eric's shiny car had new dents on its bright yellow hood and scratches that zigzagged all around to the passenger side reading "ASSHOLE." I guess my brother moved on from painting murals to working metal sculptures. I told Cindy what happened yesterday, and she couldn't believe it.

CINDY: But he was so nice! Except that day at the mall.

ME: Yeah. Well, I guess Sandra thinks he's really nice too.

CINDY: I can't believe she would stoop so low. I mean we were all friends. At least for a little while. You just don't break girl code. It was pretty bitchy of her to do it. I mean you would expect something like that from Georgina, but not Sandra.

ME: Actually, I think Little Payasa wouldn't do that. She's a chismosa and a bitch most of the time, but she doesn't seem like she would do that.

We kept talking about it, and the conversation kept going in circles, but it was okay. I didn't want to admit to Cindy that, though my heart was broken, it wasn't as broken as I thought it would be because I kind of like Martin. I feel bad about that, like I'm supposed to be lying in bed distraught, eating an entire container of Chunky Monkey. But I already did that last night. And I think one night of crying for a guy I-think-I-really-like-but-am-not-so-sure-about-anymore is enough. I'll have to sort those feelings out.

I saw Eric at lunch, and we hadn't had a chance to talk. I hadn't told him I had seen him with Sandra or anything. He was super pissed about his car. I couldn't blame him. I mean, he just bought it. Maybe Beto shouldn't have done that. He was going on and on. When I was just like *Oh, that sucks* and *mmmhmmm*, he asked me, "What's wrong with you?" I didn't say anything. And he knew there was something wrong.

ME: There's nothing wrong.

ERIC: Obviously there is, or you would be more worried about my car.

ME: Well, okay. Here's the thing. I don't like you anymore, and I don't want to be your girlfriend.

ERIC: What?

ME: Yeah. I don't like you anymore. Here's the ugly necklace that you gave me.

ERIC: What? Why are you doing this? (He looked like he was about to cry, and I kind of felt good about that. My mom is right: I am bad.)

ME: It's over. (I got up and walked away. And because I watch a lot of telenovelas, I added, in the most dramatic way possible...) By the way, I saw you at the mall yesterday. You made a mess all over the carpet with your ice cream.

He, of course, couldn't say anything.

December 5

The weirdest thing that happened after I broke up with Eric is that Joshua Moore came up to me and asked me if I wanted to go to the movies with him on Friday. Joshua Moore asked ME to the movies! ME! I would have been an idiot if I said no. I've had a crush on him like forever! Okay well, I kind of stopped having a crush on him a while back, but he's still super duper HOT! I told Cindy and Sebastian, and they said it was a stupid idea to go out with him. They asked if I had forgotten that he had gone out with Sandra? Of course I hadn't. Though when he asked me, I was so hypnotized by his beauty that I did forget. But of course I couldn't admit to that unless I wanted a whole lecture on inner and outer beauty. I asked my mom if I could please go out with him on Friday night to the movies. She told me to ask my dad. (My dad? Really, Mom?) Finally, I convinced her to let me go.

My mom hasn't been herself since she's been pregnant. She doesn't look too fresh. She has morning sickness and some sort of diabetes, and she's been losing weight instead of gaining it. Tía Bertha is being nicer and trying to help out, but she's a little too much sometimes. Like she wants us to pray with her now that my mom is pregnant, and my dad is being, well, my dad. But she doesn't want us to pray to the Virgen or to saints or anything Catholic. We are not the type of Catholics that go to confession on Friday and mass on Sunday. We are more like the "there's a bautismo on Saturday and your grandma will be mad because we didn't show up, so we better be there if we don't want to hear another lecture on how my mother is letting us go straight to hell" type of Catholics.

My abuelito used to say that we live like los animalitos, because we did not have our first communion and my parents lived in sin, not being married and all. Not by the Catholic church at least. My mother wanted to take me out of the animalito stage and make my grandfather proud, even if he was dead.

The second step for me to morph from animal to human was taking me to the church youth group (which I quickly ceased attending and wish to forget ever happened because all it did was fill me with questions and guilt). The beginning step had been my first communion a few years ago, but I don't think my mother's that committed. My aunt is different though. I think she just wants us to join in her Hallelujahs! and Amens! that can be heard all the way down the street. That ain't happening. We met in the middle and agreed to pray in separate rooms so religions wouldn't collide.

December 7

Can't wait until my date with Joshua this Friday! It's going to be awesome! I bought a new outfit for the occasion. It's this super cute red skirt which was kind of short for my usual style, but Cindy threatened me into buying it saying that it looked really cute on me, and if I didn't get it she would tell my mom about my stash under the last drawer of my dresser. So I got it. I also bought this black top and black tights and cute little loafer things. I can't wait! Even though she went shopping with me, Cindy keeps telling me that going on this date is not such a good idea, and I reminded her that her track record isn't so good. She wasn't too keen on that comment.

The thing is that high school boys are *young, dumb and full of cum.* That's the saying, I think. Santa Maria High School is not an exception to that rule. We have all kinds of boys: The Good, The Bad, The Sweet and The Jerk. I love them all...well, some more than others. I...we (Cindy and me) are boy crazy. I guess Cindy can no longer be boy crazy, so that just leaves me as the crazy one. And not ashamed at that. Well, a little. Because girls shouldn't be boy crazy, right? That's what my mom always says. She says that we don't want to be faciles—easy, sluts, hoes or ofrecidas. And that being this way was what got Cindy in trouble, and, unless I want to follow in her footsteps, I should think twice about going out with Joshua.

She says she knows that I'm young, and I'm probably confused, but that I can't go from one boy to another. "Oh, que te crees? Americana? We don't do things like that." My mom is a trip. Her friend Amelia recently divorced her husband like three months ago, a man she had been married to for twenty-five years, and she's getting remarried to some other guy—who happens to be twenty-three—next week. Amelia, I reminded my mother, is as Mexican as they get, unless Oaxaca is now a part of the United States. She said it was different, and I didn't know what I was talking about. That's her answer every time I am right about something that she doesn't like me being right about—"You don't know what you're talking about because you're still a girl." Sure, Mom. Besides, I told her, I wasn't going from one boy to another. And it's true. I am not Joshua's girlfriend, and I am definitely not Eric's girlfriend anymore, so I am free as a bird. She said that girls are never free. They always have to comportarse bien. Behave well. Ugh. She said she wouldn't stop me from going out with Joshua, but that I would regret it. "Vas a ver que tengo la razon." I hope she's not right. I don't think she is. What could happen that would be so bad?

December 8

I will never find out what could have been so bad about going out with the incredible edible Joshua Moore because that ass-face canceled on me. He said something about having to start work on Friday and how he was really sorry, and he would make it up to me and blahbity blah blah. My mom didn't say anything about Joshua standing me up, although she could have. She could have said something about me pacing around like some desperate hyena, waiting for Sandra's leftovers. Well, she wouldn't say that because that's not something that my mom would say, but I guess that's how I feel. What possessed me to believe that Joshua Moore would ever want to date me? A fat girl? I had already imagined that our night would have gone like this: I would have worn my new outfit, the red skirt and black blouse. He would have picked me up and would have had a box of Scotchmallows from See's Candies. Just Scotchmallows, none of that milk chocolate truffle crap. He would also have had tulips. Bright pink tulips. We would get into his Toyota pickup and drive off to the new Frida Kahlo exhibit at the Santa Maria Museum of Art, where we would stroll around, talking about each piece and contemplating the amount of pain the poor woman was in as each stroke was made. Then he would take me to that cupcake place near the museum, Cassidy's Cupcakery, (where I got diarrhea from Cassidy's famous sugar-free coconut cupcake that time I was on one of my many diets, but I wouldn't have told him that part in case the poor boy might be disgusted, and I certainly would not have ordered the sugar-free coconut again) and we would have dessert before dinner. Then we would go to the Pizza Shoppe and eat three slices of pepperoni pizza (each). When he would drop me off, he would give me a soft kiss on the lips and look longingly into my eyes and tell me how he had been waiting for me for so many years, but was so intimidated by my sheer awesomeness that he had never dared approach me.

But—that scenario was not in the stars. Instead, I will be at home working on my spoken word poem about my dad and scarfing down more of my creamy disappointment remedy: Chunky Monkey Ice Cream.

December 9

My disappointment didn't last too long. During our poetry class this morning, Martin asked me if I would be interested in workshopping poems together. I was like, "What?" He said that he was working on some poems at home that were not assigned by Ms. Abernard and would I mind helping him with them. I was a little shocked because Martin is a poetry genius. Why would he ask me? But I said yeah, that it would be cool, in a monotone-kind-of-uninterested-sort-of-way. I mean, what else could I do? Get all excited and giggly and say with gusto (hmmmm I wonder if I am using that word correctly? Usually I only use that word when I'm talking about food), "Oh my God, Martin! Please come on over. I secretly have a major crush on you that I won't admit to anyone, not even Cindy or Sebastian, and you coming to my house would be a fantasy come true!" Yeah, that would probably be a bad idea. However, I did say something like, "Oh my God, Martin! It'd be cool to work on poetry with someone else. And I have some really good beef jerky we can snack on!" Which, now that I think about it, sounds pretty awkward and creepy. Who gets excited about snacking on beef jerky, no matter how good it is? Me, that's who. And only me. Oh well. Tis the life of a misunderstood teenage poet. But maybe it didn't sound so bad to Martin because he said that sounded good. Also, Ms. Abernard had been explaining that there are groups of people that get together and work on poetry and that some of us should consider joining or starting such a group. Hopefully, he thinks that's what I was all excited about.

Two people that weren't so excited about my pseudo-date were Sebastian and Cindy. I had to bail on Cindy's mom's green enchiladas. Her mom makes the best enchiladas verdes in the world. Apparently Cindy had been craving them and since her mom is finally getting used to her daughter being pregnant (and is a little excited about being a grandmother), she is fulfilling Cindy's every food wish. Sometimes I wish I was pregnant just to use the "I'm eating for two" excuse. Though I know that excuse is bullshit, and Cindy will be regretting all the tortas de carne asada she's been downing. Her mom is still disappointed in her of course and still makes inappropriate and hurtful comments and still says that it will take her a long time to forgive her for what she did to her, but, besides that, she's been a peach. When I told Cindy and Sebastian that I wasn't going to go over because I was going to work on poetry with Martin, they were surprised.

I tried to play it off like I was doing Martin a big favor while secretly I couldn't wait to have him in my clutches. "Yeah, we're going to work on some poetry. He's been having trouble with one of his poems, and I said no problemo, I'd be glad to help. Besides, I'm working on a poem about my dad and he said maybe he could help me." When Sebastian said, "Really? You're going to ditch us for stupid poetry with Martin?," I was a little hurt. I tried not to let it show, but I think he realized that his words had cut a little. Not deep like a machete, but sting-y like a papercut. "Sorry, Gabi. It's just that you've never turned down Cindy's mom's enchiladas. It's just weird, that's all. I guess if you want to meet with Martin instead of us it's fine, but..."

If that's what you want is friend talk for you-shouldn't-want-that-and-if-you-do-you-are-somewhat-of-a-traitor-so-you-best-be-changing-your-mind-now. But I didn't fall for it, though I tried to make it seem like it was a really hard choice. "Sorry, guys, but I already said I would meet up with him, and it'd be rude if I didn't follow through. I don't want him to think I'm a flake." Following through is something I've been working on. In any case, Martin should be coming over in like an hour.

December 10

Yesterday was the best date ever! Okay, so it wasn't a date in the romantic sense, but it was an amazing date on the calendar. Martin came over around 6:00 p.m. For some reason, I didn't mind him visiting me at my house probably because my dad has been gone for over a week, and it doesn't seem like he'll be back for a while. I saw him at the park the other day, and I know he saw me too, but he just turned and walked away with some of his homeless friends. My mom would be working a double shift tonight at the hospital, but she said that Martin could come over since my tía Bertha is still hanging around, and she definitely wouldn't let any hanky-panky go on. Beto was teasing me because I think he knows I like Martin. He asked, "So who's coming over?" when he saw me take out my good beef jerky stash and some soda.

"Martin."

"Who?"

"Martin. He's this guy in my poetry class, and he wanted to work on some poems together."

"Hmmmm. How cute. Two geeks sharing poetry. Hahahahaha!"

"Shut up! It's not even like that!"

"Really? Then why did you take out your so-called "good" beef jerky that you won't share with anyone?"

"Whatever."

I walked to my room, but I could hear, "I thought so!" as I closed the door.

Everything was ready when Martin got there: the beef jerky, the sodas, my heart, hopes and expectations. Tía Bertha let him in and said we could work in my room as long as the door was left open. She wouldn't let us use the living room because she would be watching the news and then novelas. I don't mind novelas so much (okay, secretly I love them) because they are full of over-exaggerated drama and acting. In real life, if anyone behaved like they do in a Mexican soap opera, we would think they were insane. We went to my room (I was so thankful my mom made me clean it up!) and sat on the floor.

MARTIN: You're room is pretty cool. Why do you have so many pictures of Zac Efron on your wall?

ME (totally blushing): Well, they're old posters, and they've been up there for a while. I kind of had a crush on him when I was a freshman.

MARTIN: Oh. Well, it's okay because I used to have pictures of Eva Mendes on my wall.

ME: Ha!

MARTIN: So did you send out any college applications?

ME: Yeah. I sent out a bunch. I hope I get accepted to at least one.

MARTIN: Me too. I can't wait to go to college. I mean I love high school, seeing my friends everyday and having easy homework, but there has to be something more.

ME: I know what you mean. I really want to leave this one-horse town. Last year we visited a school in San Diego, and I loved it! It was cool, but my dream is to get into Berkeley.

MARTIN: Dude, I went on that field trip too! I didn't know you were there. Can you imagine picking your own classes? Being able to take classes that you are actually interested in, not stupid AP calculus or AP anatomy physiology. (I stayed quiet because I didn't have either of those classes and felt a little stupid.)

ME: Yeah, I know what you mean. (I popped a piece of jerky.) Jerky?

MARTIN: Hey, this is pretty good. I thought it was kinda weird when you mentioned it, but it's actually tasty.

ME: It should be. I get it flown in from Mexico. (Okay, I know that sounds a little show-offy, but it was true. My tía, who lives in Mexico, sends it by mail and the mail takes a ride on a plane. Ipso facto, I get it flown in from Mexico.)

(He looked a little impressed. And I looked a little more embarrassed, suddenly realizing that my brother was right, and I had an unnatural obsession with beef jerky. Oh Gabi, you are quite the catch. *Sheesh*.)

ME: Anyway, should we get started on the poems? I'm almost done with the one about my dad. I just need a title and the last stanza needs some work.

MARTIN: Okay. How about we switch them like we do in class?

So we did. Martin's poem was good, though not one of his best. I think my poem was better, but of course I didn't tell him that. His was a pretty sad poem because it turns out his mom died when he was eleven, and the poem was about all the things he remembered about her—her voice, how she smelled, what she wore, etc. The reason that it wasn't his best was because some of the words he used were too cliché: heart, soul, love, cascade. Those words are too overused in poems, and Ms. Abernard warned us against using them. Strangely enough, the poem I wanted to work on was about my dad dying because of his drug addiction, and I didn't feel embarrassed sharing this with him. Martin said it was an "awesome" poem, and that I should definitely read it at The Grind Effect. I told him we should go together, and he should read "La Llorona." He said we could go after Christmas break, and I said that would be super fun. And then he said, "Cool, it's a date" with a big grin. And that's when I just about lost it. A DATE! A DATE! I just agreed to a date with Martin Espada, my secret crush.

We finished working on our poems around 10 p.m. Because my tía Bertha was still watching her novelas, she didn't even notice or mind. And we actually did work. Who would have known that writing a poem would be so much work? And that I would actually use a thesaurus for something other than vocabulary flashcards? Something actually useful? I sure didn't. But it was worth it and I was happy with the finished product. Martin even helped me with the title.

IN LIGHT OF THE FEAR OF MY FATHER'S DEATH I WRITE THIS DOWN

An occurrence
occupies a space
between thoughts
lies prostrate professing something
strange gurgles gurgle underground
in a wasteland
of waiting
twiddling thumbs
twiddle dee twiddle dee
and tapping fingers
tappity tappity tappity
waiting for his collapse,
callous?
Maybe.

But you don't know my dad.

He's antagonized with life.
Breathing causes anguish.
He spits in God's face
and waits for a reaction.
Rejected—
Not even God responds
to his plea.

It is an act of faith
that fathers him,
that sets a place
at the table
but
what if faith forgets one day?
What then, old man?
Where does that leave us?

I write this down erratically,
fashioning fathoms phantoms
half a league half a league
and onward we trudge.
He grips my hand and forces
the strike
the keys click click away
the pen whistles on the page.
But he
does not know this.

Considering considerations of things
and of spaces
and traces of men
masculinity and machos
of springs and winters
wasted and waiting
and nothing again.
Again, I sound anticipatory.

But you don't know my dad.

He's a pill popper,
a consuming alcoholic,
the daddy daddy
that drifts from
funny to mean
and back again,
is back again.

Guilt of gluttonous
consumption
on corners
corners him.
He evades questioning questions
and dodges disagreements,
a refugee in refuge
a reduction of
my father the brave.

I don't want to
write this down
or speak it true.

But you don't know my dad.

A man like this
constructs time
to wait
and it waits
a watered-down vision
volatile
vicious
vehement in victory over existing or letting exist.

It is not enough,
his own breath
to inhale.
He will take yours.
I've seen it happen.
Just ask my mom.

A cast set
in iron or wood
splintering
cracking
breaking
not able to hold
not able to hold at all.

His words, a rush of
fire
inflamed flesh
that drips

like
Pollack
against always against
something.
A canvas
of pine,
of cedar,
of cherry or maple,
materials his hands
have molded,
nailed,
built,
created,
erased,
eradicated.

He is a beautiful man.
I mean that plainly.
But what more can I say?
I am his daughter.

Distraught thoughts pound
and endless guessing of what's to come
from the meth man.

Honor thy father?

But you don't know my dad.

Addiction allows
our arrival
here
to this
space.

This justified jest,
just what
I needed to justify judgment,
to cast stones,
my finger pointed
and aimed
at the gut.

It is a bloody mess.

But you don't know my dad.

December 25

Christmas went surprisingly well. Every year I am afraid that something
bad will happen like my foot being run over or my dad puking all over the
presents (again) or our family getting dressed up to go somewhere and, as
we are walking out the door, my dad deciding that we're not going after all

because he doesn't feel like it. Or us actually making it to our destination, but my dad saying "I'll wait in the car" which is code for I'll-wait-in-the-car-until-you-guys-go-in-and-then-I'll-go-and-get-high. But this year, this year, everything was perfect.

My dad didn't even get high. We went to my tío Humberto's house. He's always a lot of fun to be around, except when he gets really drunk and wants to dance with me. I hate it when he does that because then my mom forces me to dance with him. She says, "No seas haci, he's your uncle. Get up and dance with him." Which is easy for her to say because she doesn't have to deal with his drunk breath or horrible dancing (which is more like stomping on cucarachas than actual dancing). And it's not like tío Humberto only wants to dance one song—oh no, he has to dance at least four or five and all of them with a beer in hand.

But tío Humberto didn't get super drunk this Christmas. I think it's because he has a new wife who doesn't put up with all that shit like his old wife did. Or maybe he's just actually happy now. In any case, Christmas was great. We had a lot of tamales, buñuelos, and my favorite Christmas drink: ponche. I wish we would have ponche all year round. I love how the smell of boiling guavas, apples, tehocote, cinnamon, and sugar cane fill the house. I must have drunk like five mugs full. Just writing about it makes me want some more. Maybe if I ask my mom really nicely, she'll make some.

Mmmmm...ponche.

We rocked baby Jesus at midnight on Christmas Eve (it was his birthday of course—it's not all about tamales and ponche), said some prayers and then opened gifts. This year I got lotions from my tía Lourdes, one of those big bouncy exercise balls that older ladies use for flat abs from my tío (thanks for the hint), clothes that I picked out and wrapped from my mom and dad, a nice drawing from Beto and a box of chocolates from my cousin Lourdes (she knows me too well). The chocolate didn't have a chance of making it home. I love Lourdes, I wish I could see her more often, but since she went off with her boyfriend to Texas, I only see her during holidays.

We survived AND enjoyed Christmas—a rare occurrence in the Hernandez household. But I am grateful. Next up: New Year's. My fingers are crossed because tía Bertha will be present. She didn't come to tío Humberto's because she doesn't believe in our sinful ways and instead went to her little cult—I mean church—and celebrated the birth of Jesus with them. They probably sacrificed a goat and drank its blood. Ha!

December 26

I can't believe what happened today. Cindy and Sebastian came over so we could all exchange gifts (we have to wait until the 26th since we can't see each other on Christmas because Christmas is family time at all our houses) and were in the middle of our third leftover buñuelo when my mom said, "Gabi, te llego halgo. You have something in the mail." Which was weird because I never get anything in the mail. So I went to see what she was talking about.

It was a medium-sized brown box. When I tore it open, there was another box inside, and so I tore that wrapping and uncovered a red gift box with a card on it. I got a nervous feeling in my stomach which was not buñuelo-related.

"Who's it from?" my mom, Sebastian and Cindy were eager to find out.

The thing is, so was I. But I had a feeling who the gift was from, and I wanted to open it in private so I could have my own true reaction without having to be embarrassed and harassed about details and "Why didn't you tell us?" type questions. I opened the card and realized it wasn't signed. The card had a picture of a jolly-looking Santa Claus on the cover, holding a sack of toys. On the inside it read, "Ho ho hope you have a Merry Christmas and Happy New Year!" It was very generic.

"It's not signed," I said, a little disappointed. "I don't know who it's from."

"Lame," Sebastian said.

"Open the box! Open the box!" My comrades were anxious.

I opened the box and found a bizarre collection of things, none of which seemed to fit together, but all of it made me smile. There was citrus-flavored beef jerky, Scotchmallows, a purple T-shirt with a black stencil of Edgar Allen Poe's face on the front with the word "Poet" beneath it (it looked totally homemade), a Moleskin notebook, some fancy gel pens, and a book of poems by Pablo Neruda. I couldn't stop smiling. I still can't stop smiling! The chismosos that were watching me open the gift were a little shocked.

"Oh my gosh! You totally have a secret admirer!" Sebastian was really excited about the prospect.

"A secret admirer that knows you a little too well. Sounds more like a stalker to me." Beto had apparently been watching the scene unfold and had to ruin a perfectly good moment with a cynical observation. "How does this person know that you're freaking obsessed with beef jerky? And nasty ass chocolates? It sounds like you should be watching the bushes outside, making sure no one is standing there with binoculars or in your closet waiting for you."

"Thanks, Beto, always so positive."

"Ay mijo! Obviously, there's a boy who likes your sister and cares about what she likes. Now imagine if she lost a little weight and took more care of herself, how many more boys would like her?"

Thanks, Mom, way to kill the buzz. I took my stuff to my room and Cindy, Sebastian and I finished opening our gifts. Cindy got me a box of Scotchmallows and a new pair of earrings with little blue owls on them.

"Had I known Secret Lover Boy got you the chocolate, I wouldn't have."

"I can never have too much chocolate, and I love the earrings! They will make the perfect addition to my collection," I told Cindy.

Sebastian gave me and Cindy the same gift: a framed picture of us outside my house. This was taken the day after we had all sent out our college applications, which is why we look so happy and relieved at the same time. In the picture you can tell that Cindy is pregnant.

"I wanted each of us to have one. Then no matter where we go, we can take it with us so we don't forget where we came from or what we've been through. And I know Cindy doesn't like to have pictures with her pregnant belly showing, but you know what? Who cares! Everyone knows you're pregnant, and that's part of your life now and part of our life. I don't want us to be ashamed anymore (we all were crying by this point) of being pregnant or gay or poor or having a crackhead dad! I want us to be fucking proud of ourselves. This picture was taken right after we sent out our college apps—how many kids who are unpregnant, straight or rich can say that? Okay, maybe rich kids can, but who can say they did most of it on their own? Not a lot. So we have to be proud and always remember who we are and when we make it to college, who we were."

"Oh my God, Sebastian, you are so corny! I love you so much!" We all hugged like some lame group of kids in a scene from a stupid feel-good movie. But it was okay because we all were feeling pretty good, and I think we all really needed a hug. When they left, I opened the card again and looked at the back. On the back, in blue ink, Martin had written a haiku:

Gabi green sea eyes
siren softly calling me
and deeply I fall in

December 31

New Year's Eve. My dad is missing. The beast has taken him, I am sure of it. I am brought back down from my Martin-high to Gabi-reality. I guess having two happy holidays in a row, plus receiving an amazing Christmas gift from the boy I have a huge crush on, would have been too much of a good thing. And we can't have that happening, now can we?

January 2

We picked up my dad at the hospital. Someone found him in the park bathroom. Thank God for good Samaritans even if they did steal his wallet.

January 10

We came back to school today. I didn't know how to act around Martin, for various reasons.

ONE: I was 99.999999999999% sure it was him who sent the package. BUT...what if it was some weird crazy stalker who was lurking around trying to find some fat-Mexican-teenage-writer-type to stalk, and he happened to come across me, and now he is lurking in the bushes, and one of these days he'll take me and throw me in a hole somewhere where other girls who look eerily like me will be whimpering and waiting for death in the same Edgar Allen Poe T-shirt that the creepo made? I ran that scenario by Cindy, and she said I needed to stop watching so much *Criminal Minds* and that maybe I should focus on finding out who really sent the package.

TWO: I wore the Edgar Allen Poe T-shirt today in the hopes that Martin would say something like, "You got my gift! I'm glad you liked it. Do you want to be my girlfriend? Maybe we could get some tortas?" And I would say, "I loved the gift! Yes, I'll be your girlfriend! And I know of a really good torta place!" I didn't run that scenario by anyone.

But when I wore it, all he said was, "Nice T-shirt" and whether I was still up for going to the coffee shop. I said yes and he said, "Cool, you wanna go Friday with Lindsay and me?"

Fuck. Fuck. Fuck.

Why would he send me this stupid T-shirt if he and Lindsay are making all sorts of poetry sex plans? Well, there was nothing I could do to save face except accept the invitation anyway.

"Sure. Is it okay if I bring Cindy and Sebastian?"

"Yeah! The more the merrier!"

I asked Cindy and Sebastian if they wanted to go and both of them said yes. Cindy said she definitely would because she only had two more months before she was condemned to solitary confinement.

I said, "No exageres. Relax, I'm sure there are plenty of baby-friendly places you can go to."

The rest of the day I felt bummed. And then each time I passed by a mirror or window, and I would see the T-shirt that could or could not be from Martin, I felt even shittier because I would remember how good I felt when I opened the box, and then I would remember how bad I felt when Martin exposed the torrid love affair he is having with Lindsay.

Why does this fat girl have such bad luck with boys? Ugh. Time for a churro.

January 12

My mom said I could go to the poetry reading on Friday with Cindy and Sebastian as long as I take my brother to his friend Epifanio's house. Epifanio sounds like a strange first name for a kid to have, but add Smith as a last name, and you totally blow peoples' minds. I guess that's what you get when you have a White dad and a Mexican mom who doesn't care what anyone else will think as long as the name of her father, grandfather, and great-grandfather is passed on.

Epi (as he is known to the rest of the world) is nice enough, but I know for a fact that he, Miguel, and my brother still go around tagging. I've tried talking to my brother, but he says to mind my own business. What he doesn't get is that he is my business. I know I am only like two years older than him, but I still worry about him. And I worry about my mom and the stress he would put on her if he were to get arrested again. Why can't he think about that? I mean she is pregnant, after all.

Not to mention the wrath that would rain down from tía Bertha. I already had to listen to her go on about the poetry reading and how horrible it is that I'm going. She says that a nice young woman does not expose her thoughts like that to the public. That writing is something that only men should do, like going to college. She still hasn't wrapped her head around the fact that I *am* going to college (I hope). She said that what I should be doing is losing weight and learning how to cook and clean so I can catch a good husband. I don't ask her why, if she has followed her own wonderful man-getting-advice, she wasn't able to keep her own husband and insists on sleeping with someone else's—even if he was her husband first. I feel like saying "Como chinga con eso! It's not like you're Miss America, Tía," but I imagine I would get slapped in the face so I don't use those kinds of words when addressing my aunt. I swear, sometimes my life feels like it's straight out of a telenovela.

All I need to have happen is to find out that this family took me in when my rich mother abandoned me on the doorstep of this house because she had had an affair with the butler, and her family said she had to get rid of me, or she would be disowned. But that will never happen—I look too much like my mom for that even to be a possibility.

I'm still feeling bad about Martin and Lindsay. The worst part is that since I haven't told Sebastian or Cindy about my liking Martin, I really have no one to talk to about it. I think I'll tell them tomorrow. I don't know why I haven't told them, I guess it's just something that I wanted to keep for myself. A secret for me. Wow, that sounds really lame. Good job, Gabi.

January 14 (actually January 15th at a ridiculously early time in the morning)

I was so wrong, so wrong, so super wrong, about the situation between Martin and Lindsay. I have to start from the beginning so that when I reread this journal in my old age, I will look back and laugh at how dumb I was.

Thursday in the morning, I told Sebastian and Cindy about my crush on Martin, and they were like, "We know. We were just waiting for you to tell us." I asked them how they knew, and they said that it was obvious because I was always talking about how great his poetry was and saying things like, "You should've heard what Martin said in class today, it was hilarious," or "Martin's poem about the trees rustling in the wind was really profound," and other ridiculous things like that.

I had to think about what they said for a little bit, and then I laughed really hard because when I thought about my conversations with my friends in the last few weeks, the majority were Martin-related. AND...both of them suspected that he had been the one who sent the Christmas box.

Sebastian said, "Only he would send such a corny gift." AND Cindy said she ran into him at See's Candies when she was buying my Scotchmallows, and he too was buying Scotchmallows.

"The only problem is," I said, "that I don't know if he was the one who sent the gift because he asked me to go to the poetry reading first as a date, and then he said he was going with Lindsay. What kind of date would that be?"

"Lindsay?! I totally thought she was super nice and sweet! What a two-faced bitch!" Cindy did not hold anything in.

I love having friends who have my back, even though it means judging someone on something we are not too sure about.

"I know. Me too, but I guess we were wrong."

We spent the afternoon talking about the not-nice things that Lindsay had done, like laugh at Sebastian when he was eating a hot dog a little too sexy, and he started choking. Although we all laughed at the time, now we realized it could have gotten ugly, and wouldn't it have been a strange thing to have to explain to teachers and paramedics: "Our friend Sebastian was demonstrating that he could shove a big sausage much further down his throat than his friend Cindy, and that's what caused him to suffocate on said hot dog." Yeah, it would have been totally embarrassing. I felt bad for talking about Lindsay like that because she had always been super nice to me and always gave me good comments on my poems, but I felt like it was the Sandra and Joshua Moore situation all over again. I went home, did my homework, ate some leftover caldo de res (twice because my mom's beef stew is the best), took a shower and went to sleep. I didn't even feel like writing in my journal.

The next day (technically yesterday), Martin was excited about going to the poetry reading...and so was Lindsay. I tried to pretend like I was too, but the truth was I didn't feel like going anymore. During poetry class, Martin and Lindsay came and sat next to me and started making plans.

"So I can pick you, Cindy and Sebastian up if you want. I am taking my mom's van, and it seats seven people. Lindsay will be going to my house, and so she'll be with me when we leave."

"Sounds good," I said, "Except that I told my mom that I would drop my brother off at his friend's house, so I guess I'll have to take my car."

"Where does he live?"

"Over off Fifth and Oleander."

"Well, that's on our way. I can drop him off."

"Okay, that's cool. If you really don't mind." What else could I say?

At 7:30, Martin picked us up. Lindsay was sitting up in the front and offered me her seat, but I said it was okay. We dropped off Beto and headed towards The Grind Effect. When we got to the coffeehouse, there was a group of college kids hanging around, smoking and drinking really black-looking coffee. My anxiety level went way up. I don't know what I expected, but I guess Martin sensed that I was feeling super anxious and held my hand.

HELD MY HAND!

He said that I would be fine and not to worry. My head started spinning, and I didn't know what to say except, "Won't Lindsay be mad if she sees you holding my hand?"

To which he replied, "What? Why? She's gonna meet her boyfriend here, and my aunt asked if I could bring her."

They're cousins! I am such an idiot. After that, I felt a bit more relaxed until I saw that Ms. Abernard was walking up to us.

"You made it!" Martin was not surprised to see her here.

"You knew she was coming?" I asked.

"I invited her." He was smiling.

"Are you poets ready?" Ms. Abernard asked.

"I guess so. I'm a little nervous."

"You'll be fine, Gabi. Don't worry." She reassured me. But I was not so sure.

The area where we were about to read was underground. The lights were dim. Red couches lined the walls and there were plastic folding chairs for the people who arrived late. First up to the mic was a college girl talking about sex (which—guess what?—was super awkward to listen to since our teacher was sitting next to us) and then it was some guy with a poem about weed (more awkward moments) and before Martin was some hippie-looking guy with a didgeridoo. I didn't even know what a didgeridoo was until he brought out this really long horn thing and started playing music on it—if you call that music. Which I don't. It sounded more like a whale in a lot of pain than a song. Martin went up, and he read his poem about his mom and everyone cheered. Some people even cried. I was one of them.

I was up next. I almost didn't want to go up. I was really nervous. Finally I got up, and I read the poem about my dad. My hands started shaking as soon as I stepped to the mic, but then something happened about two stanzas in. I got so lost in the poem—and in getting all the emotions out that came with it—that I forgot where I was. Cindy and Sebastian were surprised and proud. They told me they would try never to make fun of poetry again.

Afterwards, Ms. Abernard said, "You were great up there, Gabi. Never stop writing. You have a gift that many would like to have. Don't ever give up on your writing, it would be a waste."

I told her that I wouldn't. By the end, it didn't seem too weird to be sitting at a coffee shop with our teacher. She almost seemed like a regular person.

Almost.

Lindsay went home with her boyfriend so after Martin dropped Cindy and Sebastian off, he took me home. All we could talk about was the reading and all the weird college kids. I asked him to stop at the stop sign near the elementary school around the corner from our house. I couldn't help myself, and I leaned over and kissed him. I KISSED HIM. I broke one of the cardinal rules of being a girl. Again. I didn't wait for the boy to make the first move. He was shocked, just like Eric had been. I waited for his reaction. He leaned over and kissed me back. It was the best kiss ever. Better than kissing Eric and probably one hundred times better than kissing Joshua Moore would have ever been.

"*Ummm*. So, yeah." He smiled.

"Sorry, I couldn't help it. I'd wanted to do that for a long time, and if we had kissed in front of my house, my mom would be watching through the curtains, and I didn't feel like getting yelled at."

"Don't apologize. Please. I had been waiting a long time for that kiss too. Waiting since before you went out with Eric and before Joshua Moore asked you out."

I felt my face turn red. "Uhhh...," was all that would come out of my throat.

"So...uhhhh...would you...like to be my...novia?"

I laughed a little. I hardly ever heard Martin speak Spanish so it was cute to hear him.

"Yes. I would love to be your girlfriend, Martin Espada."

And we kissed a little bit longer until a car came up behind us and honked.

He dropped me off a few hours ago, but I still can't sleep. Can't stop smiling. It has been the best day of my life. The best part was the poetry. I mean kissing Martin was a close second, but nothing could beat the high that reading poetry gave me. Ever since Ms. Abernard had us memorize "anyone lived in a pretty how town" by e.e. cummings that first week of school, my life changed. I'm going to write a poem about it. I have to get it out.

POETRY READING

Hands shaking
fast talking
speaking
reciting
these exciting words
in that underground coffee shop
with the older crowd
who are cooler than me.
Cindy snaps the shot
the flash threw me off
I smile and hesitate
start again.

Offer it up for sale there
my fat girl words
in my fat girl world
take it I say,
you want it?
I got it here for you,
all of this for all of you.
Spitting words
saliva dripping down my chin now from all that speaking.
Poetry is a nasty, dirty business.
Poetry makes you sweat,
each word you write is like that
first kiss you dreamed of
and I imagine
the first time you have sex.

Ms. Abernard got me hooked.
Old hippie lady
long gray hair
big round glasses
flowing skirts
who smokes in her car at lunch
the stench permanent on her home knitted sweaters.
She taught me about e.e cummings—
that dead white guy changed my life.
Before him it was rhyme rhythm rhyme
it was punctuation
capital letters and teachers saying, "THIS is a poem."

"anyone lived in a pretty how town"
she says, read it, memorize it, and we will discuss it next week.
It was all wrong.
all lower case(even his name!)
Now I sleep with cummings
dream in words
think in meter
and spit up ink.

I can't stop writing.
I write about trees.
I write about love.
I write about my brother.
I write about me.
I write about my mom.
I write about my dad.

And it helps.

Poetry helps heal wounds.
Makes them tangible.

At the poetry reading I read
a poem.
A prophecy I wrote down.

Almost couldn't go through with it.

But it came out
hurried and hot
and by the end
my tongue was on fire.

January 17

Going to school this morning knowing that I am Martin's girlfriend feels so good. But I don't know what that will be like. Will it be like dating Eric? My feelings for Martin are different (I think). What does he expect of me? What should I expect of him? What should I expect out of myself? Am I thinking about it too much? Probably. I need to chillax and go with the flow.

After school...

It was an awesome day. I can't believe that a few months ago I was all upset over some stupid guy who didn't really care about me. I told Cindy and Sebastian what happened when Martin dropped me off. They of course were excited for me. At lunch we all sat together and talked about the coffee shop and how the college kids weren't embarrassed to talk about sex in public. I mean it's one thing to joke about it with your friends but a totally different thing to talk about it in front of strangers. I have no problem talking about sex with Cindy and Sebastian. Like Sebastian told us about how he practically had sex with Pedro. Well, I guess he did because going down on someone probably counts as sex. Although I think that's pretty gross. I mean guys pee from there! Ewww! I told Sebastian that, and he just laughed at me. Cindy says she really can't remember what happened with German. She says she remembered it hurt but that it felt good too and that it didn't take as long as you see in the movies, and it wasn't as neat and clean as you see in the movies either.

Sometimes I hate being a virgin. I hate not being able to share things too. I think that Martin could be my first. I really, really, like him. But I don't know. What if he thinks I'm too fat to look at naked? I mean I think I'm too fat to look at naked. Jiggly bits and pieces. Too many rolls. My legs are thin, but I wish my thighs didn't touch. Ugh. I need to do something about this weight.

I have to go. Dinner time. And then homework. Too much homework.

January 23

It's my birthday today! I turned eighteen. Cindy and Sebastian came over to celebrate. And so did Martin. My mom made me my favorite: sopes. I love sopes. There's something so satisfying about the thick little tortilla-like discs, topped with carnitas, lettuce, sour cream, queso fresco, and my mom's super spicy green salsa. Cindy, of course, did not have green salsa. Neither did my mom because they apparently get heartburn because of the alien inside of them.

My mom bought my cake from a lady up the street who makes the best cakes in the world. They are so moist and delicious that it doesn't matter that she hasn't been approved by the city health inspector. Beto came out of his room and had sopes and cake with us. He even got me a present—a new journal to write in which he had "decorated" with all sorts of graffiti. It is actually really beautiful. I could tell he took a lot of time on it. It meant a lot to me. Cindy got me a really nice pen with my name engraved on it and a line from my favorite Sylvia Plath poem, "Lady Lazarus:" "And I eat men like air." She said, "I wanted to get the whole stanza on there, but it was too expensive." Sebastian's gift was a framed picture of me at the poetry reading. He had each person who was there write a note and put it behind the picture. Even Ms. Abernard wrote a note.

"I know it's another picture, but I thought that this one would be special just for you."

Then I opened Martin's gift. It was an autographed book by Sandra Cisneros. SandraFREAKINGCisneros. It was signed to me! It was her collection, *Loose Woman*, and it said, "To La Gabi, on the loose!" I just about wet myself.

"How did you get this?!" I think I shouted.

"Well, last week she was at my cousin's college, and I asked him if he could get it for me, and he did. I thought you would want it. Don't worry, I would have given it to you even if you had decided not to be my girlfriend. I'm glad you like it."

My dad is home, looking really bad, but at least he's home. He gave me a hug, and I could feel his ribs. Then he handed me a small box. In the box were two things: the first was an itty bitty doll. Ever since I can remember, my dad has been bringing me quarter-sized dolls from who knows where. I have them all saved on a shelf in my room. It's a strange little collection to have, but they're cute so I've kept them all. Also, they remind me that he still thinks of me. The second thing was a gold necklace with a little pink-gold-topped golden cupcake. Where this came from I don't know and didn't ask. My last gift was from my mom. It was a cell phone!!!! I am so excited! I have once again entered the 21st century. She said that I couldn't use it to make long-distance calls (I don't know anyone long-distance), and if I went over my minutes I'd be in deep shit. Well, she didn't say deep shit but the Spanish version of deep shit. I was so happy, I ate another sope. As a matter of fact, the food was so good, even my tía Bertha came out of hibernation.

She's been locked up in her room, super bummed because her novio/

ex-husband Tony told her she couldn't come see him anymore because his new wife is pregnant, and he doesn't want to ruin that relationship. I overheard her telling my mom and dad last week when I was supposed to be asleep. I heard the door open at like 2 a.m., and it was her. My mom told her that that's what happens when you sleep with someone else's husband. And that "eso" (which is code for "sex") is all that men want from you. And once they get it, then you are worthless to them, and they don't want you for anything and then, "Ya no sirve uno para nada." Nobody is going to want you now.

That was hard to hear—my mom really thinks that all of our worth is between our legs. Once a man has access to that, then we are worth nothing, and there is no future for us. I wonder if that is why my mom is so unhappy. Does she think that since she slept with my dad and never got married (at least in the Catholic church) that she is stuck with him for the rest of her life? That no one else would want her? That is really sad. There are several questions I want to ask my mom. I made a list of them.

QUESTIONS I WOULD LIKE TO ASK MY MOTHER BUT AM
AFRAID TO BECAUSE SHE WILL PROBABLY THINK I AM: A)
BAD, B) WHITEWASHED, AND/OR C) ALL OF THE ABOVE.

Do I have to get married to be happy?

If I like girls instead of boys, will you still love me?

How old were you when you had sex for the first time?

and

    a. Were you scared?
    b. Did it hurt?
    c. Were you pressured?
    d. Did you feel ashamed?
    e. Was it with someone you loved?
    f. How did you know you were ready?
    g. If you weren't ready, why did you do it?
    h. Weren't you embarrassed taking your clothes off?
    i. Did you feel fat?
    j. Did it feel good?
    k. Did you bleed?
    l. Did you still talk to the boy afterwards?
    m. How many boys or men have you slept with?
    n. Do you regret any of it?
    o. If I touch myself, will I go to Hell?

Why do you tell me that sex is bad, but you tell my brother to use a condom?

Why do you teach me to be independent but tell me that I need a man?

What if I don't want children?

If I don't like beans, does that mean I am not Mexican enough?

Why are you always telling me to lose weight if you don't?

Why do you always compare me to other girls like Sandra?

Do you know that every time you point out how much weight I have to lose, I love myself less?

Do you know that when I try to talk to you, you never listen?

If I do not like makeup or dresses, does that make me less of a woman?

If you think I am so smart, why do you think I will make stupid choices?

Why do you think you are weak if it has been you that kept our family together?

How will I know when I'm a woman?

I think my mom needs to read Sandra Cisneros' poetry. Especially her poem "Loose Woman." That's the kind of woman I want to be when I grow up. That's the kind of woman I wish my mom saw herself as.

January 26

Algebra II is kicking my butt again. I am barely pulling a C. If I don't pass this stupid class, I can say good-bye to college. Martin tells me not to worry, that I can do it. That's easy for him to say because he's a math genius (especially for a word guy), but for this fat girl it's like eating soy ice cream—completely unbearable. Okay, well, math isn't that hard, but it's boring. I hate it. Sebastian said he'd tutor me and I'm going to take him up on his offer. I'm going to ask him if we can go tomorrow after school. We could go to Pepe's House of Wings and have some wings. I love wings. Sigh.

Now that I have my phone, I can text anyone anytime I want to, although I kind of miss the old landline. But I guess this is better because I don't miss my mom listening in on my conversations. On Fridays, I stay up late and talk to Martin until like 3 or 4 in the morning. Once or twice,

I've heard my mom come towards my door, and I've had to hide my phone under my pillow with my beef jerky. It's worth it though.

January 27

Worst study session ever. Sebastian was awesome—he is a human calculator and has the patience of a saint, but I should have picked somewhere else to study. I was overwhelmed by the lemon pepper goodness that is the lemon pepper wing, and so me and Sebastian just ended up ordering a bunch of wings and calling Cindy to join us. Then we bought a pizza and each of us ate a slice of flan. Pepe's House of Wings is an eclectic mix of Mexican and Italian and wings (whatever they are). My test isn't until next week so we have some time to study.

February 3

This would be the part of the movie where the father dies, and the daughter loses control, and she goes on a self-destructive rampage, sleeping around and using drugs (like her father), always searching for what she lost when she was just a teen. But this is not a movie. This is flesh and blood. It is slow motion. I cannot move. I float above myself and get an aerial view of the tragic end. In a corner of our garage, my father had found refuge chasing something that he would never find again. He is slumped. Pipe in hand. Tip broken. A reddish residue had made a beautiful pattern in what is left of the glass. My first thought was, "Dad, are you okay?" I think I spoke those words out loud to him. But of course he wasn't okay. He didn't answer. Didn't move. Fear consumed me. I had dreamed this very scene many times before. Sometimes even hoped for it to happen in those moments of despair when I was wanting to know where my dad was even if it meant that he was gone. But in those brief moments, it wasn't like this. I had imagined relief. But this is nothing like relief. I see myself standing over him for such a long time that my feet grew roots next to the washing machine. I heard something say, "Move, Gabi, move." I ripped my feet from the ground and knelt next to my dad and shook him. My father. My papi. But he was gone.

I reach in my pocket, pull out my phone, dial 911.

"911. What is your emergency?"

I cannot speak. I've gone numb.

"911. What is your emergency?"

I know I have to answer but can't.

"Are you okay? What is your emergency?"

Finally, words fall out of my mouth.

"My father is dead."

"Excuse me?"

"He overdosed. "

"What is your location?"

"8767 N. George Street. Santa Maria. We're in the garage."

"I will transfer you to the Santa Maria Fire Department. Please hold."

After the call, I sit there. Holding my dad's other hand—the one without the broken glass. I haven't held his hand since I was a little girl. And now I realize if I had gone into the garage earlier to do my laundry, like I had planned...if I hadn't decided to watch the stupid novela with tía Bertha...if I had been there earlier, my dad would be alive. His hand was still warm. I don't remember that I haven't told my mom until the paramedics arrive. She is confused when they show up, and then she's not. She breaks down, and I think she screams and cries but sounds are muffled. Tía Bertha holds her and holds herself together. She has imagined this scenario also, but I'm sure it didn't feel like this to her either. Someone moves my dad and pulls my hand away. I sit there. They try to revive him. Rip his shirt open. Do everything possible. I want to scream, "It's no use! He's dead! My dad is dead!" Instead I turn away. Beto is at the door. I stare up at him. He sits down next to me, and we cry. Holding each other like when my parents would fight, and we wanted to feel safe.

February 4

Autopsy.

February 6

Wake. Awake. A wake. What does that mean? No one is awake. Especially not my dad. There was a box and a body in it. I forced myself to look inside the box. Even after my mom told me I shouldn't. But I didn't want to remember him the way he was in the garage. Some day, I will find the mortician who fixed my dad up and thank him. The body resembled my dad, but it was like an old version of my dad. There was color in his face, more brown and less yellow. His long black hair was tied into a very neat pony tail and tucked in behind him. I hadn't seen his hair combed for months. No long homeless-man beard, no mustache. I touch his hands. I shouldn't have. No dirt under fingernails. There was an earring I had forgotten about in his left ear. The scars from all the scratching, barely visible underneath the makeup. Rotted teeth hidden, somehow his mouth seemed full. The clothes were clean but too large for the man wearing them. It was an old white suit I had seen in a photograph my mom has from an anniversary dinner years ago. I almost wanted to laugh. Really, who buys a white suit? My mom does. He hated the suit, said it made him look like he was about to have his first communion. But he wore it that one time for my mom, swore he would never wear it again. "Ni muerto." Those were his exact words—not even dead.

February 7

The funeral was surreal. At the service, we were asked to say some things about my dad. About his life. So I tried.

"My father was born in Sonora, Mexico in 1972. He came to this country to make a better life for himself and my mother. He worked with his hands and was very smart. He could have been an engineer. Or a doctor. Or an inventor. He was funny and kind and always willing to help someone. If your car was broken on the side of the road, my dad would stop and help you. Even if my mom got mad. In fourth grade, when I tried to make my mission out of sugar cubes and realized—only too late— that when you put glue on the cubes they would dissolve, my dad went to his truck, took out some tools and wood and helped me build a better one. He knew about cars, construction, and plumbing. He was the best whistler I've ever met. And yes, he was a drug addict. And yes, he overdosed. Let's not pretend this is something it is not: that we are here because my dad lived a long happy life. Because that would be a lie and an insult to my dad. He did not live very long, and he was rarely happy, at least recently. But that doesn't mean he was a bad man. He was a very good man who made very bad choices that ended up killing him. There are many people sitting here today who took advantage of my father's kindness, of his giving spirit. Who knew he was an addict and took advantage of him. You know who you are. I bet you're feeling guilty or sorry so I won't say anything else about that, except that it's a bit too late for guilt or apologies. He's dead. And I miss him. I miss his jokes and his guitar playing and his hugs. I want—"

I couldn't tell the people listening what I wanted. I burst into tears and ran. Ran down the street and kept running until I found the spot, curled into a ball and cried. In the evening when the stars still came out, and the moon crept through cracks in the ceiling, and cars drove by, and the neighbor kids played tag in the street as if nothing had happened, as if nothing had changed, my brother dragged me out and locked the garage door.

I don't think I'll ever get out of bed again.

February 10

Tía Bertha walked out the door. Tired and a little older. More worn out than when she arrived. Prayers didn't work their magic. The flaming tongues of the Holy Spirit failed her. Had God taken back her gifts?, she wonders. Her faith is in limbo. She could not save her little brother.

"Maybe this is punishment for what I've done with that man. Maybe it was really a sin." Just like my tía to believe that God only thinks about her.

February 12

"¡Ya parate! Get up!" Mom banged on my door. Opened it. Sat on my bed and waited until I turned around. Her eyes were red. I haven't thought about her once. About the baby that's on the way. A baby who will never know our father. Never know anything but that he overdosed. I haven't thought about Beto. Cindy and Sebastian went to the funeral and came to see me a few times but left after we sat in silence for more than an hour. Martin also came. I didn't feel like seeing him. I guess I am bad after all. My dad died, but I never thought about how he was my mother's husband. The person who knew her best, the person who she married in a small church in a small town in another country. Who helped her cross the border through hills and migra and dogs and rivers. Who taught her to drive. The person who she was supposed to live with forever was beginning to rot in a hole three blocks away. And we can't do anything about it. "Ya estuvo bien. That's enough. We can't stay in bed." Then she says what I didn't want to hear. What I was hiding from. "Tomorrow you go to school." "I can't, Mom. I can't. I hurt. Me duele. Todo me duele." I cry again because it's true, everything hurts. She holds me. I am five again. Crying on my mother's lap. Knowing if she holds me, things will get better. Beto comes in. He says something for the first time since I found our father in the garage. "Laying in bed won't bring him back. Stop being stupid. And get up. That's enough, Gabi. That's enough. We have to get up." Mom holds us together as we both fall apart.

Where do we go from here?

February 13

Never having experienced popularity in any shape or form, having eyes on me was unnatural. Annoying. Cindy and Sebastian were my wall at school today. They protected me, deflected questions meant to hurt. Stupid questions like, "Is it true you found your dad?" and "How do you feel?" "Well, just peachy. Found my dad overdosed in a corner in our garage, pipe still in hand. I feel superb. Never better. What kind of stupid fucking question is that? Are you an idiot?" But my real answer is always, "Good." Most people don't know what to say (the best thing would be nothing), and I forgive them. But Georgina, who is queen of the idiots and therefore not "most people," makes a comment only the queen of the idiots would make—"I didn't know your dad was a crackhead." Before Cindy could say, "Shut the fuck up, you stupid bitch!" (which she had started to say), I slapped Little Payasa. Hard. My hand left my side before I could tell it to stop. Luis, the security guard, saw it all and turned his back to us. No one said anything as I walked away. Luis had known my dad since he had come to this country twenty years ago when they both worked at a warehouse as security guards. I felt relief. Who would have known? All it took was slapping someone in the face.

February 18

I forget and wait for him to come home. I dial his phone. *The number you have dialed is no longer in service. Please hang up and try again.* I listen to his voicemails. Just to hear his voice. The one from my birthday last year when he was doing really good. The one when he forgot where that street was in that city where he had a new job. The one from a few months ago when he called and left a funny song. The one from a month ago asking for money. The one from a few weeks ago saying he was sorry, crying, and asking for more money. All of them. I just want a piece of him—even if the piece is in sound.

Martin says that eventually I have to move on. I have to be there for my mom and for my brother. And for myself. He says that when his mom died, he stopped talking for two months, and he would sneak out of his room at night and watch videos of her. But that slowly life moved on. And he had to do things because he thought that maybe his mom was a ghost and that she would be really upset with him if he didn't do his homework or clean up his room. He learned to be a good person because he had a fear of upsetting his mom's ghost. I told him I was sorry that I was so mean to him, and he said that I didn't have to apologize. That everyone grieves in their own way. Grieve: a word that I never thought would apply to me.

February 22

My teachers have all been extra nice and have let me turn in my work late. Should I even care about school anymore? Is that fair? How is doing schoolwork at a time like this grieving? Martin has convinced me that it's important. Cindy and Sebastian both said, "Don't be ridiculous. What are you going to do? How would becoming a super senior make things better?" They're right, it definitely wouldn't make things better.

None of my poor teachers, however, know what to say or do. So, instead of addressing the ghost of the meth man in the room, they ignore it. Now there's an awkwardness in all our conversations. I bet most of them have not had to deal with those realities. I bet my dad probably asked one of them for money in one of their fancy shopping centers. Or maybe he was kicked off one of their nice little streets by the police. No one addresses that ghost except Ms. Abernard. She tells me to write about it, that writing helps, that her dad killed himself—shot himself in the head—when she was fifteen. "And if I can survive that, Gabi, you can do it better. But you need to write. Don't let your anger and sadness sit." She breaks the school rules—and hugs me as I cry all the tears I've been trying to hold back at school.

February 23

I don't know if I can write anymore. I want to lift my pen, but it's heavy. Almost like the tip is chained to my desk. I think about the poem I wrote for my dad and wonder if it's true what I wrote. Did my dad really want to die? Were we not enough for him? Was this world not enough? Or was it too much? I try to remember happy memories with him. Riding on the back of a horse, him teaching me to ride a bike or him letting me paint the dollhouse he built for me. But even those memories are tainted by words my mom says or by the things I leave out and then remember I left out. I still cry myself to sleep. Cindy and Sebastian have been the best friends I could ever ask for, but I know they can't understand what it feels like to lose your parent. Sure, Sebastian doesn't talk to his dad but not because he's turning to dust a few blocks away. It's not the same. Even Georgina's stupid ass apologized for being so stupid. But I didn't apologize back. That would have been hypocritical. I will though. I really shouldn't have slapped her in the face.

February 24

Trying to write at least a piece of a poem everyday.

> Roses are red
> violets are blue
> sugar is sweet
> and now you have diabetes.

February 27

It's getting close to Cindy's due date. I didn't think it would actually happen. I mean, obviously it had to happen, but I guess I hadn't imagined how real this would be. It's strange how time keeps going on. My dad died, but babies are still being born. Cindy's gotten so big she can barely walk. She has to do independent study now because she's tired all the time, so I don't get to see her at school anymore. I try to stop by and see her at least three times a week though and give her all the chisme of what's been going on at school. Like how Georgina got caught having sex in the emergency exit stairway with none other than Joshua Moore (who seems to really get around), and her parents had to go pick her up. How embarrassing! I would have loved to have been a fly on the wall to watch it all go down. Not to watch Georgina and Joshua do the wild monkey dance but to watch them getting caught. Although I feel a little sorry for Georgina. Her dad is an asshole. I should say, "Well, now she'll know what she put Cindy through," but being treated as a pariah is not something that anyone deserves—especially for having sex because everybody does it. It sounds cliché, but sex is a natural human function. I mean we shouldn't do it with everyone, but maybe it isn't as bad as parents make it seem. But what do I know, I'm just a virgin. Both Joshua and Georgina were suspended for a few days, but what could the school really do? They're also not supposed to be talking to each other—ha! Like that's going to happen. Adults are incredibly naive sometimes. "Ojos abiertos, piernas cerradas." It sounds so simple. But it's not. Maybe when my mom was young, no one had these feelings between their legs that are supposed to be forbidden. Maybe they did just speak to each other from opposite sides of the fence or on a porch under the watch of eagle-eyed chaperones. Fat chance. That sounds like another unlikely adult-constructed scenario. Because if that was the case, there wouldn't be so many young parents or parents who have never been married or divorced or kids in foster care. Young people have always had sex. But no adult will admit it. They set up rules about how we should behave without realizing that sometimes it doesn't matter what they say. If we want to have sex, we will—at night in the back of some car or in the middle of third period on the emergency exit stairway.

February 28

Beto. My brother. I love him. He used to say he hated my dad, but I knew it was bullshit. Last night, or this morning actually, he got home drunker than a mother. He had thrown up all over the one shoe that was left, had a busted lip and a black eye. A loud banging on the door woke us up, and when we opened the door there was Beto. Lying on the ground. My heart stopped when I saw all the blood on his face. I felt a panic attack coming on. And then it was too late. I started hyperventilating and crying. My mom just about lost her mind. It took me a while to calm down, and when I finally did I realized he was breathing, and I dragged him inside.

He started heaving. When I realized he was going to throw up again, I brought the trash can and put his face in it.

"Why he'd do it, Gabi?" He was slurring, but I knew what he was asking. "Why?"

"I don't know, Beto." I had learned that there is no such thing as having a meaningful conversation with an intoxicated person. The whole time my mom sat slumped on the couch. When she saw that I had a handle on things, she went back to bed. Her feet dragging, our unborn sibling weighing her down.

> HAIKU FOR MY MOTHER
> What is left now that
> The hungriest one is gone?
> Only heartache soup.

March 1

My brother's shenanigans sent my mother into labor a month ahead of schedule. After I showered and put my brother to bed, I was so tired I knocked out immediately. I must have been in a deep-Mr. Sandman-induced-sleep because it took my mom smashing her favorite vase against the living room wall to wake me up. My mom and Beto must of been at it for a while because, by this juncture, my mom looked like she was ready to smack him. And then she did. Over and over again her closed fist came down on my brother, who was trying to burrow deep into the wall where the vase had hit, hands covering his face. My mother, with her long hair flailing to the rhythm of her desperate beating, must have forgotten she was pregnant. Her tears matted her hair to her face. She looked so sad that I wanted to turn away. She screamed, "That's what you want, right? ¿Quieres que te peguen? Well, here, let me help you achieve that goal!" For a while, I watched like a spectator. As if this wasn't (couldn't be) my family. Nah, I thought. This couldn't be happening. My mom (always talking about the loose morals of White people who are on those talk shows she says she hates but obviously doesn't because she watches them every day) was in her living room—barefoot, pregnant, in a flannel nightgown—beating the shit out of her hoodlum son. If you ask me, you couldn't get anymore White trash than that. All we needed was a trailer and a crackhead father. Oh wait, we had one of those.

She kept on wailing on Beto, screaming, "You want to be like your father? You want to end up like him? I had enough of that shit! Enough of not knowing if he was coming home or if he'd be found dead somewhere, of washing blood and vomit from his clothes! I had enough! You're not going to do the same to me!"

She had never hit us like that before. Sure, we'd gotten a smack across the face a few times for talking back, but a full on mother-child-beat-down? Never. As fucked up as our family has been, my parents only used corporal punishment in extreme situations. And only to reprimand, never to inflict pain.

But even with my mom's hands coming down on him, my brother still managed to say some dumb shit, "Well, you got what you wanted! You said you'd rather he be dead! Didn't you?! Isn't that what you fucking said?!" He cussed at my mom. He fucking cussed at her. It took me a second to react, but I pulled my mom as gently as I could to separate a deranged pregnant woman from beating the shit out of her son. Because, yes, that is what my family had suddenly become. We had entered an alternate universe where we were ruled by primal urges. Of course, while trying to stop the madness, I got smacked a few times by my mother's crazy hands. Then shit got even more real, real quick. My brother apparently still had a foot in that alternate primal universe and thought it would be a good idea to come at my pregnant mother fist raised. Yup. That happened. Thank God for my catlike reflexes because I was able to push him back hard against the wall and yell at him, "Calm the fuck down!"

Defeated, my brother fell to the ground and spat at our mother, "I hate you! All you ever care about is yourself. Always! That's why he's dead! You killed him!"

She just looked down at him, greñuda and barefoot, her big belly heaving from all the excitement.

"Shut up!" I shouted. "Cállate! You don't know what the hell you're saying!"

When my mom grabbed her belly and released a painful groan, I knew we were in deep shit. I don't know how I got her to the car, but I did. Beto rushed to her side and was saying, "I'm sorry, Mom, I'm sorry. I didn't mean it. I'm sorry, Mom." And he was. But it didn't matter.

Got to the hospital and have been waiting to hear how my mom is doing. But to recap on how I came to be sitting in a hospital waiting room (hoping to hear that I am not suddenly an orphan) for the last twelve hours: I woke up to the sound of a breaking vase. My pregnant mother beat the shit out of my brother, who then came at her. I pushed my brother and cussed at him for the first time. He yelled at our mother that he hated her, which then prompted her to go into premature labor. Hernandez family bullshit: that's what's for breakfast. And that should be our motto.

I had to call my tía Bertha. I was not ready to handle a situation like this. She had moved back to the same apartment complex, three cities away, where she had lived before she had moved in to help with my dad. I explained the situation to her, and she must've flown here because she arrived in time to go in with my mom when the baby came.

March 3

Ernesto Julian Hernandez is my new brother. He is named after both my grandfathers. The two-day-old is in an incubator struggling to breathe. The doctor says he'll be okay, but since his lungs are not fully developed he still needs a little help. Beto feels super guilty. And he should. I don't want to be angry at him or blame him, but I do. If he hadn't shown up drunk and beat up, none of this would have happened. And I guess if my mom hadn't reacted the way she did, it wouldn't have happened either. So it's probably both of their faults. Though I'm pretty sure that soon I'll be blamed for this incident. But we can't stay mad at each other with our new brother in a plastic box. And I guess no matter what, we're still family, even if we don't want to be. Yay, family, she said sarcastically.

Cindy and Sebastian came to see him. Cindy looked so tired. Before she left she said, "This baby needs to hurry the heck up. I feel like crap. My mom's been making me walk around. I can't really sleep anymore. It doesn't matter what side I try to sleep on, I just can't sleep." So she only stayed for like fifteen minutes, but I was grateful that she did. Sebastian brought Ernie a little rainbow bear who he had named Jeff. It made me smile. Martin just left like an hour ago and brought Ernie a book by Dr. Seuss, *Oh the Places You'll Go*. That guy is just so optimistic. I think I love him.

March 4

Ernie will be in the incubator for another few weeks.

It's March. College rejections should be getting here soon.

March 10

Balancing school and family is becoming a Herculean labor. But, unlike the young demigod, I haven't killed my family, and I am sure there will be no gods or goddesses trying to help me cope with all my woes. What I do have are friends, but they have their own problems and lives, and I cannot be weighing them down with all my sadness. Cindy is about to pop, and it would be unfair to stress her out. Sebastian is trying his best. He's joined the LGBTQ club at school and is really busy with that. That is actually a really good thing because there was only so much we understood about being a rejected gay teen. I mean, none of us are gay so we don't know what it's like, so I'm glad he has found support with other teens who are going through the same thing. The only one left is Martin. I know he loves me, but sometimes I feel like I'm dragging him down with all the drama in my life. I have to do something to feel better. Right now though, this box of Thin Mints will have to do. I love Girl Scout cookie season.

March 13

Martin helped me find a solution which did not involve bingeing on Caramel Delites or other such foods. What it does involve is getting all sweaty. Ugh. He said he was tired of seeing me moping around and on edge all the time and suggested we start running together. He said that there was something about running that released endorphins and gave you something he called "runner's high." Interesting, I thought.

But because I don't exercise, at first I was like, "Do I look like I run? I don't keep this slim figure by working out, pal."

He didn't think that was so funny. He said that if I wanted to feel better, I needed to get serious. He told me to be ready tonight at 5 p.m. He would pick me up and take me to the park. This is the thing: I'm fat. I don't want to be fat for many reasons, mostly because it's embarrassing climbing stairs and having little old ladies rush by you while you have to pause and catch your breath. Also, there's lots of clothes I'd like to buy. It seems like when you go to the store, the only clothes that are on sale are skinny girl clothes while big girl clothes are regular price or super expensive. I wonder if it's because they have to use extra fabric? Hmmmm...well, in any case, running is an exercise that leaves you exposed—all my goodies and bits and pieces will be bouncing up and down for the whole world to see. I don't want to tell Martin this because I am afraid he'll think I am being superficial. And I guess I am, but I still don't want him to know that.

My good-Gabi side, the one who wants to get fit and healthy and doesn't want to feel depressed anymore says, "No one is going to be looking at your goodies or bits and pieces. And if they are, so what? Focus on your goal and get to gettin'." But the bad-Gabi, the one who doesn't give a shit about anything, says, "Run? What are we, athletes? Ha! Don't worry about that, love yourself for you. It doesn't matter that you can't climb stairs—that's what elevators are for! Relax, serve yourself some diet Coke and some of what you have hiding in your underwear drawer. As a matter of fact, I saw that Mom bought some chocolate chip cookies—what the hell are you waiting for?" For some reason, Bad Gabi has a lot more to say than Good Gabi. And she is usually a lot louder and a lot more convincing.

In the end, Good Gabi beat up Bad Gabi, and I went running. Martin was right: I felt better afterwards. I felt a sort of euphoria even though my heart was about to jump out of my chest, and I was as red as a lobster. Martin said, "That's a runner's high." Never having been high myself, I am taking his word for it. Whatever it was, I felt better.

March 14

Ahhhhhh! Cindy went into labor! The alien she's been keeping in her belly is about to claw its way out of placenta, mucus, and tissue! Or just pop out of her vagina. In either case, there are two people allowed in the room with her, and she let me be one of them. The other is her mom. I am about to witness the miracle of life.

Later...

That was freakin' gross. Much more disgusting than anything I could have imagined. I wish I had been in health class the day they showed us those videos. Had I done that, I would have been prepared for the show that Cindy's reproductive organs put on for us tonight.

First off, there was a lot of screaming. A lot less than in the movies, but much more than what I thought there was going to be.

Secondly, there was a lot of sweating and pushing. And a little poop. Fucking poop! Cindy had been told not to eat anything the night before, but she did. It's not like she knew she would be in labor but still. So, when she was on the table pushing her heart and baby alien out, something else came out too. Out of a different hole. Which meant that I saw my best friend take a crap in real time.

The whole thing was traumatic. I mean, it was awesome—in the original sense of the word. Utterly awesome. For almost a year, Cindy carried this being inside of her. When it kicked, we could see it move through her belly, trying to escape. But it stayed inside of her. Then all of a sudden, there she is on a table spread eagle, her most private of private parts exposed for a whole bunch of people to poke at. And then it happened—there was an agonizing and audible POP! Suddenly, the baby's head started to come out. I felt like I was about to faint. I actually screamed (the nurse gave me a look that said, "If I wasn't helping the doctor bring this baby into the world, I would punch you in the face, you damn wuss.") But I couldn't help it—it was too much. She kept pushing and pushing, and the baby kept coming, and then she pooped, and then the baby came out. It was all covered in bloody goo and white stuff, so it really looked like a baby alien, just like the kind you would see in a science-fiction movie. And then he was wiped down and crying, and that's when I started crying. I can't understand how something so utterly disgusting can be so utterly beautiful at the same time. But it was. When Beto was born, I was too young to know what was going on. When Ernie was born, it was an emergency, and I wasn't in the room with my mom because she didn't want me in there in case she died—that's my mom, always looking on the bright side. Instead, my tía Bertha was there and held my mom's hand through the whole thing. So this is my first firsthand experience with birth. Cindy looked so happy holding her baby, like it didn't matter that we had all just seen her vagina or witnessed her pooping on the hospital bed—the only thing that mattered was that she was holding her little boy in her arms.

Hopefully, Ernie can come home soon so my mom can feel just as happy as Cindy instead of worrying about whether or not my baby brother will be able to breathe on his own.

March 15

Cindy named him Sebastian Gabriel. I can't believe it.

March 16

At school, everyone was asking about Cindy. How's she doing, what's the baby look like, what did she name him? All the usual stuff. But the people who were asking were mostly people who had talked shit about her being pregnant in the first place, so to them I gave generic responses, "It looks like a baby. She is alive. She gave him a name with more than one letter." Soon people stopped asking questions. Georgina was one of the people who came up to me to ask how Cindy was doing. I was weirded out by her sudden change of heart.

I asked her, "Why do you care? Weren't you the one who told everyone that she was pregnant? And called her a slut?" I could see that she was about to cry and that was so un-Georginalike, that, naturally, I was stunned. "What's wrong with you? You're supposed to say something like, 'Shut up, fat ass' or something like that. Why are you crying?"

"I'm pregnant."

For a moment my brain failed me. I was completely void of language skills. My face froze in a surprised/confused expression, with my mouth agape, letting a "Whaaa...?" softly break free.

And there it was: karma. Not in the, "Ha, ha! Now you're pregnant!" way, but in a sad, "Oh shit. Now you're pregnant," kind of way. Because as hard as Cindy may have had it with her mom, Georgina is going to have it worse with her dad. Georgina's family is Jehovah's Witness. They come by our house on the weekends and when my mom doesn't say, "Don't open the door!" and has us hide behind the couch, I open the door and take a pamphlet. I can tell that neither Georgina or her brothers and sisters— or even her mom for that matter—are into going door to door, but the bruises on her mom's face let me know that it doesn't really matter what she thinks. I've seen her dad hit her and her mom in public before, but I've never told anyone, especially Georgina. That would probably be humiliating. So, as much as we don't get along, I never stoop that low. If that's how her dad treats them in public, I can't imagine how he treats them in private. He'll probably break her legs if he finds out that she's knocked-up.

My vocal abilities returned, "Wow, Paya...Georgina, I'm sorry. Have you told your parents?" I didn't think calling her by the nickname I've used to make her angry all of these years was appropriate at a time like this.

Her face got all wild and crazy, and her voice cracked, "No! They'd kill me. My dad would really kill me. When he found out I had sex with Joshua, he kicked the shit out of me. That's why I wasn't here that whole week."

(I remembered wondering where Payasita had been.)

There was an awkward silence. I hate awkward silences so I asked the first question that came to my mind: "So, do you know how many months along you are?"

She said, "Like two. The time in the stairs, it wasn't the first time. But I haven't told anyone. Not even Joshua. I don't know what to do. I can't have this thing."

And then my dear nemesis, my sworn enemy for life, started sobbing. I had never seen her like this. It was against the laws of nature, and I didn't know what to do or say.

"Well, there are other options, I guess. Like adoption. Or, you know, the other thing if you really don't want it. I mean, really don't want it." Yeah, that happened today. I suggested having an abortion to Georgina during our passing period today at school. Hope my mom doesn't ask me if anything strange happened at school today. Because, guess what?—that would top the list.

I guess Georgina also thought it a strange occurrence because her response was to yell at me.

"Are you fucking serious?"

"Hey, don't talk to me like that. Don't. For whatever reason, you're telling me about this and apparently asking for advice. I'm just putting your choices out there. I'm not saying they're good choices. But they're choices. If they don't seem good to you, just have it. What's the worst that can happen? Your parents kick you out? You can go live with your grandma or something."

I mean my grandma is no peach, but even she wouldn't turn me away if I were to become a "fallen woman," as she likes to call unwed mothers.

"No, Gabi, you don't get it. My dad will literally kill me. Seriously kill me. Like, take my life. And sorry about yelling. I had already thought about doing that "other thing," but that's like murder. I can't do it. I just can't. But I don't know what to do, and I feel so alone."

I didn't have a choice (it seemed) so I did it—I hugged my sworn enemy. What was I supposed to do? I remember how Cindy felt. How I've felt before. Sebastian. How all of us have felt like we had no one on our side. And here was this person—who had been part of the groups that have pushed us out—feeling just as alone.

"You're not alone. I know we don't get along...but I don't know. Don't feel alone. There has to be a solution out there. We just haven't thought of it yet."

So I hugged her for a little bit longer until the bell for fifth period rang, and we were both late to class. I didn't mind—it was Algebra II anyway.

She didn't have to tell me to not tell anybody—it was nobody's business.

March 18

Georgina made up her mind. I was so shocked when she told me that I choked on my Mocha Frappachino. She asked if I would go with her because she didn't want to go by herself. I couldn't say no (I had been the one who made the suggestion) and told her I'd drive her. I imagine it must be pretty scary, and lots of things must be going through her mind. Things like: Will I go to Hell? What will the doctor think about me? Will God still love me? What if I die? What if my parents find out? What if people at school find out? Will I regret it? Will I be able to have children afterwards? Am I a bad person? Will this make me a murderer?

I wouldn't want to be in her shoes.

March 19

I'm freaking exhausted. I hate keeping things from my friends, and I knew they would know something was up. I am a horrible liar. To top it off, my mom didn't let me use the car because my tía Bertha needed it to go grocery shopping. She's been helping since Mom had the baby. I can't very well put up an argument to that because then I wouldn't be able to go anywhere. At school, I told Georgina what happened, and she started freaking out. There was a solution to this setback, I told her.

"We can ask Martin. He won't say anything, and he can use his dad's minivan anytime he wants."

At first Georgina was all like, "No, no one else can know." But then I explained how it was—either we ask Martin, or we can't go. She reluctantly agreed. I assured her that Martin was trustworthy and wouldn't judge her or even say anything to her about her decision. He's cool like that. So then I went to find him.

I talked to Martin, and he got very serious and pensive, but he finally said, "Yes, I'll drive you guys."

After school we headed to Stuffix, ten freeway exits away from Santa Maria de los Rosales. The drive was silent until we got to the clinic, and I asked Georgina if she was sure she wanted to go through with it.

She said simply, "Yes. I already prayed about it."

Wow. What does that even mean? Did God give her the thumbs up in a vision? Did an angel appear in a dream and say, "No worries. Do whatcha gotta do"? Whatever it meant, she was determined to take control. We all held hands as she walked in. Georgina filled out some paperwork and waited. She was so lost in her thoughts (I wish I was a mind reader) that the nurse had to call her name three times before she reacted. I thought this was a one-visit thing, but it turns out that this was only the first part of the ordeal. She has to come back in two days for the grand finale.

March 20

Oh my God! I got my first acceptance letter in the mail. It was to a private school in Orange County that I almost didn't apply to. But I'm glad I did. I had talked to Ms. Abernard about feeling like I was not worth that school. She told me that if I was going to throw the application out, I would be one "foolish" girl.

"Of course you can make it," she scolded me. "You just need to make sure to pass that Algebra II class. Get all the help you can from Mrs. Black."

Still working on that. This gives me hope that I can probably make it into other colleges. Maybe even Berkeley. Hopefully Berkeley. Sebastian asked if Martin and I wanted to hang out tomorrow with him and some guy he's been dating (I won't even get started on that issue). I told him we couldn't because we had other plans. He made a face that read *bullshit*.

"Whatever. If you don't want to hang out with me and James, then just say so. Stop making excuses."

I tried to fix it, but it didn't go well. I do have plans after all. Plans to get rid of an unwanted baby. But that is not something that I would say out loud.

March 21

I couldn't concentrate all day at school thinking about what was going to happen later. However I was feeling though, I bet it was nothing to how Georgina must have been feeling.

At lunchtime, Martin, Georgina and I left and didn't come back. This offense is big enough to have our off-campus lunch pass revoked, but I don't think the school will call our homes because a) the school knows the situation with Georgina and her abusive dad; b) Martin never gets in trouble and his aunt is the secretary; and c) the school knows that I've been depressed about my dad dying. Hopefully they'll assume that's why I left. Otherwise, if they call my mom, I'll have to be ready with a story to tell her. I didn't even tell Sebastian that I was leaving at lunch. Ugh. Now for sure he's going to be super mad at me.

We drove to the clinic, and I asked Georgina how she was feeling.

She said, "Penitent. But I've been talking to God and my unborn child about it. I've asked forgiveness from them both."

I couldn't look at her anymore without crying, so I looked out the window. It's not that I think she's a bad person, but I feel bad for her making this decision and thinking about how hard it must be for her. Like I know she feels bad about it. Really bad. But she doesn't have another choice or feels like she doesn't have another choice. Georgina must have ovaries of steel to do this. I had never thought of her as strong . Bitchy? Yes. Nosy? Definitely. But strong? Nope. It had never occurred to me that strength was needed to make this choice. I am sure that this will not be the last day she will think about it. In any case, there's no going back. She went in and took the second pill. They told her she could hang out in an empty room they had until everything came out. We waited a few hours, and I thought about the poems I had been reading in poetry class. We had read "We Real Cool" (about how cool kids are not really cool) by Gwendolyn Brooks. I liked her writing so much, I looked up some more of her poetry online and one poem kept coming to mind, "the mother." I wanted to give it to Georgina so she wouldn't feel so alone, so she would know that there are other girls out there like her, but I couldn't bring myself to do it, and then it was over, and we drove her home. Martin had to drop her off a few blocks from her house because if her dad saw a boy driving her anywhere, it didn't matter if I was with her or not, it wouldn't be good. So we dropped her off—older and babyless. But at least she was alive.

Sort of.

March 26

Sebastian was really pissed off about me leaving and not telling him. But I told him that it was a female emergency and that I really had to go. He was kind of grossed out, but he seemed to believe me.

Regardless, I am happy because we get to bring Ernie home today! My little brother is breathing on his own, and the doctor said he is ready to come home. That's the good news.

The bad news is that tía Bertha will be moving in. Permanently. I really love my tía Bertha but having her around all the time—again—is going to be hell. I complained to my mom about this. She said that she understood how I felt and that she knew that tía Bertha *es dificil*, but the fact that she was willing to move in and help with Ernie and everything else while my mom worked overshadowed how difficult (or crazy) my tía could be. My mom told me to try and be patient, that when I go off to college she will be all alone, and she needs someone to help her.

I was taken aback by this because until now my mom was against me leaving to go to college. When my dad died, I had totally forgotten I even wanted to move out. How could I leave my mom alone? I mean Beto is here, but it's not the same. Sometimes he's more trouble than help.

"Are you serious, Mom? You won't be mad if I moved out for college?"

Her reasoning for not wanting me to move out was that I probably wanted to move out to party and sleep around, and that that's not how a young lady should behave. This line of reasoning is ludicrous. If I wanted to party and sleep around, I would. There are plenty of opportunities here in Santa Maria for that to happen. And her insistence that that is the reason White girls move out is just as ridiculous! Seriously, Mom? Only White girls sleep around? Let me introduce you to my friend Cindy, to Georgina, to Tomasa, to Kanisha, and all the other non-White girls at my school who have already had sex. And guess what? None of them are in college! But some of them will be soon. Of course I just keep these thoughts to myself because she gets all angry if I say stuff like that, and her response is always, "Yes, they're acting like that because they're trying to be White." There is no reasoning with this woman.

So, because one of her biggest fears is that I will become less Mexican, she has said that the only way I am leaving this house will be if I get married, but now here she is giving me her blessing—expecting me, even, to leave. *Wow.*

"Life is too short, mija."

I came back to my room to think. I sat munching on some Hot Cheetos with lemon and Tapatio and a bottle of Dr. Pepper (my favorite thinking foods) and wondered about what my mom said and what it has taken for her to say that. Life is short—there are examples all around me to prove this. My dad is dead before the age of fifty. Ernie almost died, and he's an infant. Georgina's unborn child never got to see the light of day. That was a pretty short life. I guess I don't have a minute to lose. I need to enjoy all of it. And if that means moving away to college to do whatever it is that I want to do (I haven't decided yet), then that is what I have to do.

Maybe.

March 29

Georgina isn't the same, and I don't blame her. I think it's harder for her to cope with all the feelings because she has no one to talk to. Obviously, her mom isn't an option. If she told any of her friends, they would spread it all over the school, probably even call her a "baby killer" like they did to Samantha, that girl who graduated two years ago. After school I went up to her and told her that if she needed someone to talk to, she could talk to me. She thanked me, but said that she is trying to deal with this on her own. I didn't want to push her so I left her alone.

On the plus side, I've gotten a few more acceptances and one rejection. The rejection didn't hurt so bad because I knew that school was a long shot but I GOT ACCEPTED INTO BERKELEY! Me. The Mexican fat girl. Accepted to Berkeley! If Sebastian gets accepted, then we can go together! Ahhhhh! The sad part (the part I really don't want to think about) is that, if that happens, Cindy will be here all alone. Should I feel good about being able to leave while she has to stay behind? We had always talked about going to college together, but that was before German knocked her up and she had Sabi (a combination of Sebastian and Gabi). I don't want to think about that right now. I just want to enjoy feeling good about my acceptance.

I told Beto and my mom and my tía Bertha about Berkeley and they were happy...at first. They all knew how much that meant to me. Then I started talking about dorms, Christmas visits, calling every day, and suddenly the reality of me moving away actually hit all of them. Beto said it was cool because now he could have my room since it was bigger and how it would be "so awesome" to come and visit up there. Tía Bertha went on and on about libertinaje this and libertinaje that, like freedom only meant sleeping around. My mom wasn't much better. What happened to all that *life is too short* stuff? She said she was too emotional right now to think about it, but that she knew that she didn't want me to move away. "Plus we can't afford it." I told her that sometimes being poor and Mexican and a girl pays off. "The government will pay for everything!" But when I told my mom this, she just glared at me and said, "Humph! The government? You have a lot to learn if you believe anything they say." Then she turned to my tía Bertha and changed the conversation. Just like that. This is what she does when she doesn't want to talk about things anymore. Her go-to solution.

I was shaking with anger. But what was I supposed to do? What could I say? So I just started crying and went to my room. I laid in bed, pathetically hugging my stuffed bear for like an hour before I came to my senses. I am going to leave whether she "allows" me to or not—whether she believes that moving away will make me a bad girl or that it means that I am trying to be White. I don't care—I'm leaving. But I won't tell her that yet. Besides, I'm pretty sure she already knows.

April 3

Prom! Prom! Prom! That is all everyone is talking about. Yes sir, in one month the students of Santa Maria de los Rosales High School will show up in our finest attire to the footsteps of the oldest train station in the world (it's really not, but it seems like it is)— a train station whose sole purpose is the yearly teenage bacchanalia that is prom. I know it's probably an historic something or other. My abuelito used to tell me that he would arrive at that train station every year, along with a whole bunch of other Mexicans, to pick crops. He would say that the U.S. government would bring thousands of Mexicanos, give them a shitty place to stay, a hole to piss in, and peanut butter and jelly sandwiches for the months they stayed picking. And then, when they were finished, they would herd the workers onto the trains and send them back to wherever they came from. It didn't seem fair or just, but my grandfather said it paid more than what he would have made in Mexico, and that even if the U.S. government still owed him money, he was better off for it. I personally didn't think it was okay, but it doesn't matter—Abuelito died with the debt never being repaid. Note to self: look up the name of the program. In any case, the train station is old and falling apart. The prom committee tries to talk it up every year, saying it's "vintage" and trying to make it seem like whatever cheesy theme they decide on will classy it up (under the sea, pirates, even *Twilight* [vomit]) but alas, no matter how many sea stars and seashells you put on the tables, it is still old and falling apart. Obviously I am going, no matter how much crap I talk about the decor. I am a senior, I have a boyfriend, and I am an American. It is my patriotic duty. I've seen the movies. Also, whether anyone admits it or not, many of us are thinking, "Will tonight be the night I get lucky in the back of my boyfriend's/girlfriend's mom's minivan?" Or maybe it's just me. In any case, almost everyone is going, even Cindy! Her mom said she would take care of little Sabi for the night. She usually doesn't do that, but since Cindy is keeping her grades up, she said it would be fine for her to go out for one night and have fun. She should be back in school at the end of this month because that's when la cuarentena (I like to call it the quarantine) is over, and she is safe to go back into the real world again. I teased her about making sure she doesn't put out during prom because she might get pregnant. She didn't think that was funny.

I've been working on some haikus for Cindy—

Party time is over girl
Summer claimed you as his
In Spring you will rejoice

Girl the party is over
Summer runs down your legs
It is Spring rejoice

Girl is over party
Summer runs claiming his legs
Rejoicing in his Spring.

April 5

Ms. Abernard invited some of her old students to come by and do some zine workshops with us. Ever since we heard that the college kids were coming, we have been writing like crazy so we would have something to work on when they arrived. I wasn't sure what I was going to write until a couple weeks ago when I got my period and I remembered having *The Talk* with my mom.

In fifth grade—just after we watched the health video about how our bodies were changing—my mom decided it would be best to teach me all about my body, though she herself wasn't exactly going to be the teacher. After watching the video, everyone was uncomfortable, and we were left with more questions. Do boys have periods? Will they also get hair *down there*? How does a woman get pregnant? Is there any way I could make my boobs grow faster and bigger? I obviously couldn't ask my teacher this (the poor woman looked anxious enough that day) and I definitely couldn't ask my mom. One day though, I was laying in bed reading *Are You There God? It's Me, Margaret* (getting the answers I so desired) when she shows up with *All About Your Body*, and stealthily slips it under my pillow saying, "No se lo enseñes a tu papa," as if it was a secret that my life depended on. It was a health book about the female body. There were diagrams, see-through pictures with descriptions of what our body parts do. Those body parts which are private—and that we are told are dirty and should be covered at all times—were exposed for what they really are: body parts. Just like an arm, just like a heart, an ear, or an eye. What the book didn't explain was how cramps would make you want to roll around on the floor. Or that you would get chills so bad that you'd wish you could sleep in the sun. Or how pads feel like diapers that you are always worried are leaking all over the place. Or how tampons are much more complicated than they appear, but that's okay because if your mom catches you with one, she'll probably make you burn it and then make you say a rosary for your slutty soul. Or that not all boobs are created equal, no matter how many times you pump your arms together. Or that bodies are all different. Very different. Yes, that book left a lot of things out. I decided that my zine would have all the information that that book left out—the truth about the female body from a female point of view. Because, really, the older I get, the more I realize how full of crap that book was—no matter how big of a stupid smile the girl on the cover had. She probably hadn't gotten her period yet.

April 7

Missing my dad a whole lot today. Wrote him a letter.

Dear Papi,

Te extraño mucho. I miss you everyday. Some people may say that you're probably in Hell because you were an addict, because you gave into vice, and you hated going to church. I am not sure I believe that. To be honest I don't know what to believe. I can't think of you as an angel dressed in white, with wings and a harp. That was never your style. But obviously I don't want to imagine you burning for eternity. Maybe there are different levels of heaven and you're just chillaxing, eating some tacos and drinking a Pepsi. And finally sober. That'd be an alright heaven, actually. I hope it's like that. Some days I wake up forgetting you're gone. Like yesterday morning, I was laying in bed a little bit, and I thought I heard you whistle, but it was only Beto. It was like feeling you go all over again. I was angry and almost told him to shut up, but I guess I should be glad that I'll get to hear you through my brother. That's proof that not all is lost. As much as he tries to fight it, Beto is a lot like you: angry, quiet and stubborn. But also kind, loyal and freaking hilarious. Oh my God, like yesterday he played the funniest/meanest joke on Mom. You know how she's super scared of mice? Well, she was carrying some rice that she was about to cook and Beto said, "Cuidado! Una rata!" And Mom screamed and jumped like three feet! The rice went everywhere! Beto and I (and even tía Bertha) couldn't stop laughing. Mom didn't think it was funny though, "Hijo de tu...! Miranomas! Que chistoso! Get the broom and start sweeping antes de que te de unos!" But Beto was laughing too hard to even move. Then out of nowhere, Mom farted and we all lost it, even Mom. You would have been laughing too.

Ernie is getting big. You would have loved him. He looks like you. Big curly lashes and bushy eyebrows. He even has your big ears! I feel sad that he'll never get to meet you. I'm glad he won't have the memories of you as an addict though. I don't wish those on anyone. We'll tell him stories of how you were a hard worker, about your whistling, your wrinkly laugh and how you loved us. Someday I'm sure we'll tell him how you died. I think we'll have to. But I don't think he'll hold it against you.

I miss you, Papi—everyday. It's hard to believe that I'll never see you again. If you are in heaven, and you do have wings and the power to watch over us, I ask you for a big favor: help tía Bertha find a boyfriend! Or girlfriend. Or something. She is way too lonely and grouchy, and I can't handle her anymore! She's worse than a teenager. Te quiero mucho.

Tu hija,
Gabi

Need to finish up my zine. Have to have it ready for tomorrow.

HERE'S MY ZINE!

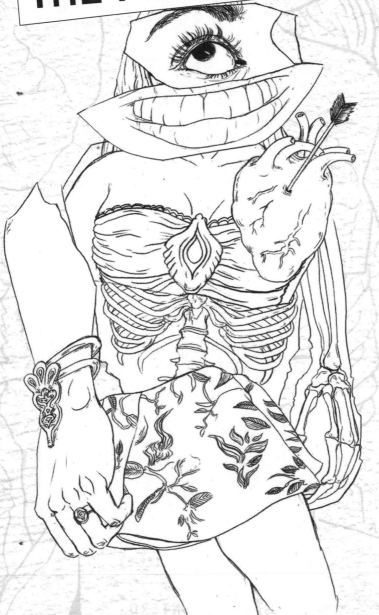

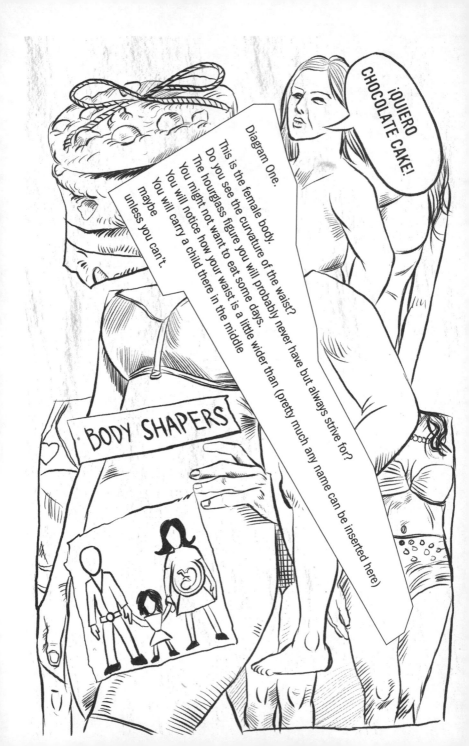

Diagram Two.

These are the breasts.
As they develop they will hurt.
You will be teased because your breasts are too small.
You will be teased because your breasts are too large.
You will be teased because you have breasts.
Boys will talk about your

tits
melons
chichis
tetas
tatas
rack
boobs

but never about your breasts.
Because breast is a dirty word.

You will want to cover them
and flaunt them
sometimes for yourself
and sometimes for others.
You may feel insecure about your breasts.
You may say things like, "I wish I had bigger boobs."
You may not.
You may say things like, "I wish I had smaller boobs."
You may not.
You may realize that you are more than your breasts.
You may not.

COME TO MAMA BOOBIES!

NG SQUA

PLUMP CHEST MUSCLES!

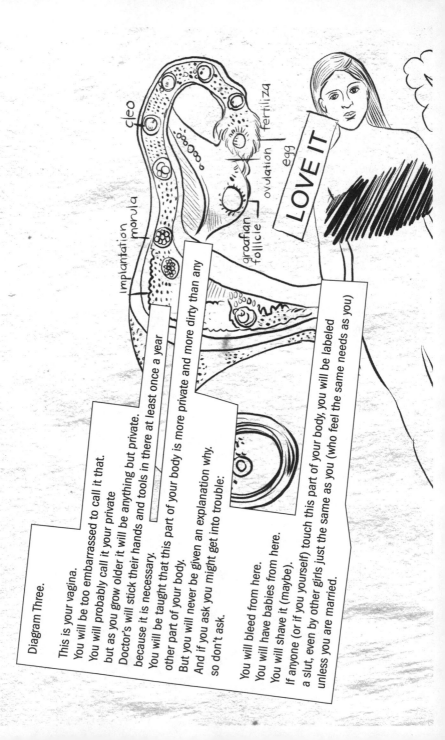

Diagram Three.

This is your vagina.
You will be too embarrassed to call it that.
You will probably call it your private
but as you grow older it will be anything but private.
Doctor's will stick their hands and tools in there at least once a year
because it is necessary.
You will be taught that this part of your body is more private and more dirty than any
other part of your body.
But you will never be given an explanation why.
And if you ask you might get into trouble:
so don't ask.

You will bleed from here.
You will have babies from here.
You will shave it (maybe).
If anyone (or if you yourself) touch this part of your body, you will be labeled
a slut, even by other girls just the same as you (who feel the same needs as you)
unless you are married.

cleo

implantation

morula

groafian follicle

ovulation

fertiliza

egg

LOVE IT

Thick Hair

DREAMING OF FREEDOM

dare to CHOP CHOP! CHOP! CHOP!

Diagram Four.

This is your hair.
Most girls have long hair.
Your mother has always made you wear it in a braid, even though you want it loose.
Your hair is long and goes down your back, because your dad does not let you cut your hair that goes down your back. And you try not to be bad.
Sometimes you will get angry because your dad does not let you cut your hair, and that is bad.
because if you do you will look like a marimacha, and that is bad.
You do not want to be bad.
Well, maybe just a little,
just to know how it feels.

So you cut it
and realize how good it feels.

You are different.

Bad is not so bad.

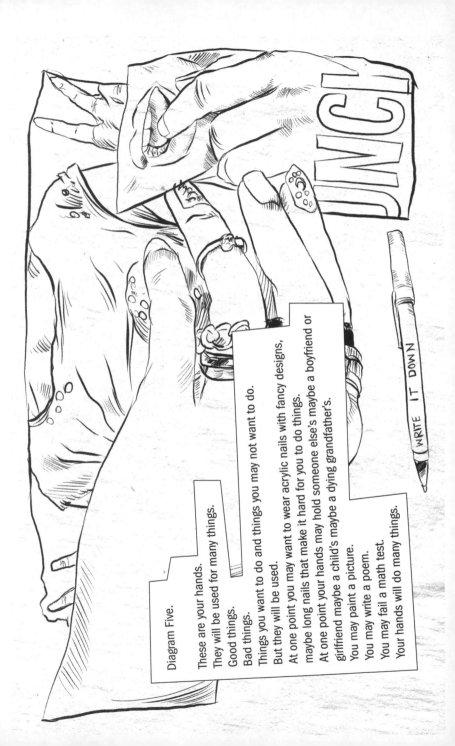

Diagram Five.

These are your hands.
They will be used for many things.
Good things.
Bad things.
Things you want to do and things you may not want to do.
But they will be used.
At one point you may want to wear acrylic nails with fancy designs,
maybe long nails that make it hard for you to do things.
At one point your hands may hold someone else's maybe a boyfriend or
girlfriend maybe a child's maybe a dying grandfather's.
You may paint a picture.
You may write a poem.
You may fail a math test.
Your hands will do many things.

WRITE IT DOWN

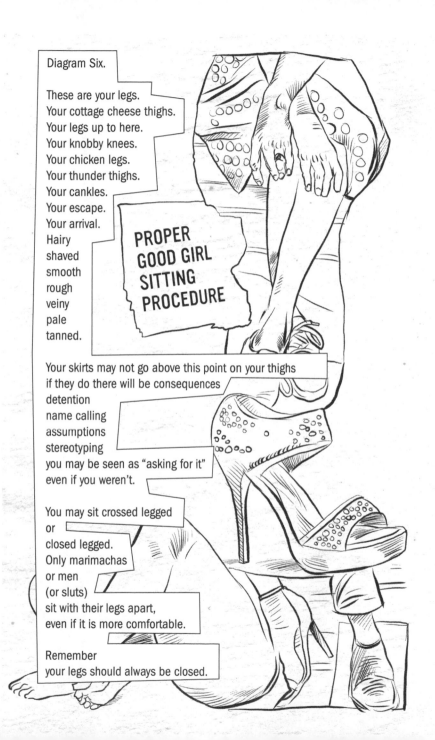

Diagram Six.

These are your legs.
Your cottage cheese thighs.
Your legs up to here.
Your knobby knees.
Your chicken legs.
Your thunder thighs.
Your cankles.
Your escape.
Your arrival.
Hairy
shaved
smooth
rough
veiny
pale
tanned.

PROPER
GOOD GIRL
SITTING
PROCEDURE

Your skirts may not go above this point on your thighs
if they do there will be consequences
detention
name calling
assumptions
stereotyping
you may be seen as "asking for it"
even if you weren't.

You may sit crossed legged
or
closed legged.
Only marimachas
or men
(or sluts)
sit with their legs apart,
even if it is more comfortable.

Remember
your legs should always be closed.

Diagram Seven.

This is your mouth.
It is made up of
teeth
lips
tongue
gums
spit
noise
curse words
moist words
sweet words
bitter words
desiccated
suffocated words
tough rough nasty tasting words.

What comes out of your mouth may condemn you.
So more than anything watch your mouth.

Giggle, keep them sweet, keep your thoughts to yourself;
you are a girl, speak accordingly.

But maybe...

You will forget all this
and learn to speak and think
and become a woman.

And think thoughts that will change what comes out your mouth.
Thoughts like:

If words are our weapons, we must ask ourselves, why should we use rocks
and sticks when we have tanks available?

And you will know how to answer

YOU OWN ALL THE WORDS IF YOU WANT THEM

Created by
Gabi Hernandez

April 8

Ms. Abernard loved my zine, but she said I definitely couldn't share it with the class because she'd get in trouble—probably for promoting critical thinking instead of preparing us for a state test or some other ridiculous reason our wonderful school district could cook up. I know she agreed with what I had to say, but I didn't want to put her job in jeopardy. So instead I am going to make another zine soon about one of my most favoritist of favorite foods: tacos. Tacos are like what the voices of a hundred angels singing Bob Dylan while sitting on rainbows and playing banjos would taste like if that sound were edible. Little bits of cilantro and onion. The perfect salsa verde or roja. Yum. Those little itty bitty tortillas holding delicate, perfectly seasoned pieces of dead pig or cow. I've got the food sweats just thinking about them. I've already started writing the haikus, and I just know that my taco zine will be hilarious.

I showed Sebastian and Cindy my female body zine and they liked it. Apparently, they were not aware of the fact that I had suddenly become a creative genius. Okay, that's not what they said. What they said was, "We didn't know you were creative like that." To which I responded with a modest, "Neither did I." I guess I've been feeling more creative recently. The more I write, the more creative I feel and the more I feel I have to share. Martin was also impressed. But what I liked most about his response was that he said he had never thought of a girl's body the way I described it. Mission accomplished. High five me! I wanted the zine to make people think about how girls are raised to think about our bodies and who gets to decide how we think about them. Like how Cindy was called a slut and constantly criticized for having a baby so young, but then it wasn't seen as that bad for my mom to have a baby because she was an adult even though she was in a really bad situation. Or how we are raised to believe that it is our job and responsibility to protect our bodies and if something goes wrong, we are always at fault, even if it's rape. And we have to fix it. Why did Georgina have to make the choice about her baby? And then live with the guilt and the fear of being found out and being labeled slut and baby killer while Joshua Moore paraded around like nothing ever happened? Like he never had an almost-child? I mean Georgina totally helped him out too—now he doesn't have a *responsibility* and is free to go and play football or soccer or wrestle bears or whatever it is he is doing to get college scholarships. And she's the one who's wracked with guilt. It makes me mad. Why are we always screwed? I love Martin, but the first time I kissed him he was surprised that I did. Just like Eric was. It doesn't bother me, really. Okay, it kind of does because if he had kissed me, it would have been the most natural occurrence, and I wouldn't have been shocked at all. I would have been all, "Awesome! This is the way things are supposed to be." Why? So my zine is about all that.

I read it at the coffee shop and the audience seemed to dig it. Afterwards Martin and I stood around trying to pass out our zines. The first people came up and asked "How much?" I wasn't prepared for that. I thought we could just give them out for free. The college kids probably explained that you could sell them when Martin, Lindsay and I were goofing around. "$1.50" was what came out of my mouth. I made $15 and Martin made $12. We are now published poets. Kind of.

April 11

Today Mrs. Howard, our English teacher, assigned groups for a poetry project—writing a mock epic. And right away people starting moaning. Secretly I was thrilled to pieces to be doing the assignment. The part that was not so thrilling was that we had to work in groups. Most students don't like writing poems, and since they know I do like writing poems, they will be looking at me to take over. Ugh. Mrs. Howard got this great idea after we read, Alexander Pope's "Rape of the Lock," where he writes about some guy cutting off a piece of a woman's hair. I waited to see what group I was in (because, of course, we are incapable of picking our own) and ended up with Sarah, Ian, and José. This is both good and bad. It is good because we get along pretty well, and those people are some of the few that are doing good in the class. The bad part is that Ian is super hot. Like super duper hot. Like he's molten magma spewing from a volcano, and I'm Pompeii hot. And I feel guilty about feeling like this because I have a super cute and super sweet boyfriend. I'm sure Martin thinks other girls are magma hot, but he's not in a group with them. Or at least I've never heard about it. Maybe he is or has been, and I don't know. I wonder what girls he thinks are super hot? Okay, Gabi, don't think about that. You will drive yourself crazy, and you are not the erratic girlfriend type. Or are you? Argh! What's wrong with me? I'm going to sit down, eat some of my Girl Scout cookie stash, reread Pope's poem, take some notes and then go for a run. Yes. That is my plan. Gabi, out.

April 13

Ernie is getting huge! I can't believe how fast babies grow and how much they eat. He is such a sweet baby too. Not like one of those annoying crying-all-the-time babies. He looks like a little round brown teddy bear, and I love holding him and squishing him and kissing his little baby belly. I think Beto is a bit jealous of the baby, but I know he loves him. He plays with him and carries him all the time, even though my tía Bertha says it is not good because if you hold a baby too much, he won't learn to be independent. But it's just so hard not to. I mean it's been a super hard year, and he's a reminder that there are good things in life too, which puts everything in perspective and makes us smile. Even though she teeters on the edge of being an eccentric old Christian lady and extremist religious zealot (that is the word of the week after we learned it in our government class when we were having a discussion about the role of religious beliefs in the attacks of 9/11), I'm glad my tía came to live with us. My mom needs someone nearby and she and tía Bertha are getting along better, even though they don't agree on a lot of things, especially religion. But as long as they (we) don't talk about God and his plan for each and every one of us—a plan that apparently does not include wearing pants or listening to rap music (I guess Lupe Fiasco is leading me down the corridors of Hell)—we are okay. Tía Bertha is a complicated person. I know she was (is?) some sort of bruja or curandera. And—while being a witch seems to contradict her current status as a messenger of God, as does sleeping with her ex-husband who is now married to someone else—somehow it makes sense. Besides, tía Bertha is an awesome cook, better than my mom most of the time. Maybe I shouldn't write that down. Although it is the truth, and my mom is all about telling the truth all the time, no matter what. So, I'll just leave it in here. Anyways, tía Bertha makes the best gorditas in the whole world. When I got home from school today, she had made those little hot pockets of masa goodness filled with chicharron en chile rojo, and there was red sauce and little pieces of deep fried pork skin on my shirt afterwards, but I didn't care because there was a party in my mouth. Not only did I have seconds but also thirds, they were so good.

I immediately regretted eating all of that gordita goodness after I spoke with Cindy on the phone. She called to see if I wanted to go prom-dress shopping with her this weekend because it was getting close, and she didn't have any idea what she would be wearing. How am I supposed to fit into any sort of non-muumuu dress after all that food? *Ugh!*

In any case, I agreed to see her on Saturday.

April 14

This morning Ian texted me, "Can you get to my house a little earlier on Saturday?"

I ignored the text. Deleted it. If it wasn't there, then he didn't send it, right? Wrong. He was standing outside the door of Mrs. Howard's class waiting for me.

"Hey, did you get my text?"

I shook my head, "Nopers. I haven't gotten any texts today, except from my mom to not forget to pass by the store after school. I think she wanted me to buy more formula because my little brother drinks a lot of it. One bottle in the morning and then one almost every hour after that it seems like. You know how that goes." No. He doesn't know how that goes, Gabi, because Ian is an only child, unless you count his older, equally as hot, step-brother Dylan. So no, he doesn't know—or need to know—the ins and outs of infant feeding habits. I could have slapped myself.

I could feel my face turning red because I am a horrible liar, and whenever I lie I turn red and start sweating and start talking way, way too much.

"Oh, well, I was wondering if you could come to my house like at 8:30. I had something I wanted to talk to you about. It's nothing big though, I just thought maybe you could."

"Sure. I think I can—if I wake up. Ha!"

And it was like someone said, "Cue the sweat!"

To make it worse, just as we are done talking, Martin walks by, gives me a card, a quick kiss on the cheek and runs back to government.

In class I read the card. On the cover it read, "O my Luve's like a red, red rose / That's newly sprung in June"—the first two lines to Robert Burns' poem "A Red, Red Rose." And on the inside of the card, Martin had illustrated the entire poem. I felt like an even bigger asshole for thinking that Ian was hot after reading it.

April 16

Because I am an idiot, I went to Ian's house early, just as he had asked. I got there at 8:35 but had been up since like 6 this morning trying to figure out what he wanted to talk to me about. I made a list:

  a) He could just want extra help with understanding what a
     mock epic was and didn't want to ask in front of the others.
  b) He wanted to practice his Spanish for his trip to Peru over
     the summer.
  c) Ian, realizing that I had a gay friend, knew that I would
     be understanding and wanted to come out.
  d) He was an avid baker and knowing that I like to eat,
     wanted to have me taste a new recipe for chocolate
     cupcakes he had been working on for weeks.
  e) He thought I was cute and wanted to let me know.

I laughed at my last one, because I am hardly his type. A short, fat, nerdy Mexican girl? Try tall, blonde, skinny athlete. It probably had to do with food or Spanish.

When I got to his house, I was in shock. Ian had money. Like real money. His parents' house was huge and very high tech. You had to drive like a mile to get to the front door and then a person (servant? butler?) let you in. It was awkward and uncomfortable. The servant/ butler showed me to Ian's room (okay, it was more like an apartment) which is detached from the house and even has its own entrance. When the butler/servant knocked on his door to let him know he had a visitor (unlike at my house where my brother just yells, "Hey Gabi! Little Ms. Teen-Mom (if it's Cindy) or wannabe Shakespeare boyfriend (if it's Martin) or Mr. Park-It-In-The-Rear (if it's Sebastian) is here to see you!"), Ian opened the door—shirtless! I instantly, awkwardly, melted and gasped out loud. Ian obviously worked out and didn't look like teenage boys were supposed to look like. He even had a tattoo on his chest! A stupid, idiotic tattoo of our high school name and mascot (a stallion) but a tattoo nonetheless. I stood there imagining what his chest must feel like. And was suddenly pulled out of my dreamlike state by his voice.

"Hey, you came!" He smiled as he pulled on a T-shirt.

I wonder if he knows how hot he is and if he had this all planned out to make me this uncomfortable.

"Yeah," I said and glanced around his room. His "room" has a bedroom, a workout room, bathroom and a den. He has a fucking den!

I couldn't believe that. I've always wanted a den. I shook my head and laughed a little bit.

"So what did you want to talk about?"

This is where my morning went comically awry.

"Why don't you come and sit over here?" He actually patted the bed. Patted the bed! Like he was calling a dog.

It was like a scene from a cheesy teen flick where the guy is about to try and convince the poor unsuspecting girl to have sex by telling her she is very pretty, then lightly brushing a strand of hair from her face, and the stupid girl falls for it even though she suspects the hot boy is after one thing that can only be found in her pants, but she has somehow convinced herself that she is different. He couldn't possibly be like that. He is way too nice and way too hot. Emphasis on *hot*.

Having gained all of this knowledge from countless hours of cheesy teen flick watching, I still went and sat my ass down.

"I know you have a boyfriend and all that, but I think you're extremely beautiful, and I really like you. I wanted you to know that I think you deserve better than Martin."

And in the midst of wondering why he thought he was better than Martin and getting lost in the sea of cerulean that were his eyes, each of them calling me in deeper and deeper...the bastard did it. He brushed the hair out of my face and kissed me. If I am being honest with myself, as this journal is the only place I can really be honest with myself, I definitely wanted to kiss him back. Maybe I did. Just a little bit, to see how he tasted. My body wanted it. Needed it. Really bad. I could feel it everywhere, my elbows, my chest, between my legs, my toes.

But, like the good semi-Catholic that I am, guilt immediately rushed over me, and I imagined my poor Martin's face hovering over us like some sort of sad ghost reminding me of my bad doings. That made me pull away. Fast. I was almost tempted to wipe my lips, but I didn't.

I was breathing a little heavily, but still managed to say, "Uhm... look...you have the wrong idea about me. I have a boyfriend. And he loves me. I mean you're hot, but I don't like you like that. Sorry."

"Are you serious?" His face lost a little bit of its hotness.

I could tell that this may have been the first time that the old brush-the-hair-from-the-face trick didn't work. He had turned red, and I could tell he was embarrassed and pissed.

"Yeah, look it was just a misunderstanding. It's not a big deal. I'm flattered, but we should probably get going because the rest of the group will be here soon, and I don't want them thinking something was happening that wasn't happening. Please."

"Sure. Whatever."

The whole morning was really awkward after that, though the group got some work done. As we walked out the door, Ian apologized. I told him it was fine, to not worry about it, it never happened. And I really did think it was fine, but I've felt guilty all day. I don't want to tell Martin because I don't think there's any point to it except hurting his feelings over something that was a stupid mistake. What I really feel guilty about is the fact that I liked how Ian kissed me. It was a very different kiss than the ones I've shared with Martin or even the ones I've shared with Eric. It was intense. The whole morning was intense. I don't want to think about it anymore. Going to take a quick shower.

Later...

Just got back from shopping with Cindy. We had a really good time, and little Sabi behaved himself. Cindy did get a lot of stares from people though, and I even heard a woman say, "Another teen mom. Her poor mother, what she must be going through. I don't know why girls today can't keep their legs closed." I totally felt like telling her, "In your day, lady, girls were sent away for getting pregnant. Or worse, they were forced to marry and condemned to be miserable for the rest of their lives." But I didn't want to ruin a perfectly nice afternoon. After looking for the perfect dress for what seemed like a hundred hours, Cindy ended up buying the first dress she tried on. But I—being the above-average weight girl that I am—sadly couldn't find anything to wear. None of the dresses I liked were available in plus sizes: they only came in "I-limit-myself-to-only-one-gordita" or "I-only-eat-lettuce" sizes. That is the main reason I hate shopping.

When I got home my mom asked how the shopping went, and I told her that Cindy found a cute dress, but I didn't because I am super fat. She said that I was not super fat, but it wouldn't hurt me to lose some weight. *Thanks, Mom.* She said that my godmother Sylvia knows a woman who sews and that it would be a lot cheaper than buying one from the mall. I felt bad because I know she's been working double shifts at the hospital where she works in the kitchen, but still we are barely making it. Even though my dad used to spend most of his money on meth, he'd still pitch in, and it made a difference. But now he's gone, and there are two more mouths to feed: Ernie's and tía Bertha's. I have some money saved up from cleaning Rosemary's house and birthdays, but I am running really low (most of it was spent on college applications, Thin Mints, and Caramel Delites), and I need to watch it if I am going to move for college. Plus, I won't be cleaning Rosemary's house anymore since her kids sent her to a convalescent home and are trying to sell her house. I couldn't believe it—I didn't even know she had children who lived nearby because they never came to visit her.

On the last day I went, she gave me some pie dishes and a box of (very erotic) romance novels. I didn't know that viejita was like that. I'm going to miss her very much. My prom dress choices were dwindling, so I told my mom I'd go see the woman who sews. Tomorrow will be my first visit with this miracle worker of a seamstress—in Tijuana. *Blah*.

April 17

Tijuana was not the business. As usual. But I will be back next weekend to pick up the dress. Red and black, mid calf. Very 1960s. Very cute. Very cheap. Very big. Very me.

April 19

Easter came and went and I didn't even notice. Since Beto and I stopped doing egg hunts, I've kind of lost interest. Obviously we are not very Catholic, but it would have been nice to know what day it was. I would have thought my tía Bertha would have reminded us, but she didn't. She didn't even go to church. She's been off lately. Off even for her.

Her and my dad were only a few years apart. I know that when they were growing up, they were very close. My dad would sometimes tell us stories about all of her boyfriends that he had chased off by throwing rocks at them or accidentally setting his dogs loose on them (this was before everyone thought she was a witch). He thought it was hilarious, but tía Bertha did not. My dad was such an animated storyteller. He'd stand up and act out the boyfriends' reactions. It's strange how I had forgotten about that part of my dad and replaced those memories with only the ones of him as a ragged man who clung to life with calloused hands and dirty fingernails. But I have to remind myself that there was more to him than that. Because there was. My favorite story he told was the one about when he was crossing the border with my tío Isauro, and they were caught by Immigration, but only because my tío was so hungry, he had eaten some warm mangoes with chili and had gotten major chorro. My dad would always laugh his ass off as he painted the picture: it was summer and the prison cells that the migra kept them in were super hot. "Everyone was sweating their balls off and your tío Isauro couldn't take it anymore! He started yelling at the guards, '¡Hace un pinche calor! ¡Dejenos salir! ¡No sean animales!' But obviously no one listened, so your tío started taking his clothes off until he was butt naked! Some people laughed and others called him a pig, but your uncle didn't care. He just lay there on the floor fanning himself until they let us go." By the end of the story, I'd be holding my stomach from laughing so hard. My mom hated it when he told that story. It was her little brother after all. But I loved it.

I think tía Bertha hasn't been able to accept that my dad is gone. Her faith tells her that my dad is in Hell because of the way he lived his life. He wasn't the best father, he had several vices, he technically took his life, and he didn't go to church. Her God—or the God her church has told her about—doesn't forgive easily and is more of a punisher and less of a lover than the God my mom has taught us about. She probably can't reconcile the fact that she will not be reunited with him in the afterlife and won't accept that her brother will be suffering in flames of eternal damnation forever. A terrible thought. Good thing I don't believe that. I can't believe that. I'd rather believe the equally unlikely scenario that my dad has somehow morphed into an ethereal entity with ultra creepy spying powers and now has nothing better to do than watch over his family, making sure that they make better choices than he did.

April 21

Today during lunch, Georgina came up and thanked me. She told me not to worry, that it had been for the better and that I had done the right thing. It took me by surprise because Cindy and Sebastian were with me when she came up to me. After she left, they had a lot of questions about what the hell she meant. And since I didn't know what to say and because I am a horrible liar, I made up some story about a burrito and spilled beans and helping her take it out with some soap in the girls' bathroom a few weeks ago. I finally fessed up and said that I couldn't tell them what she thanked me for and please don't ask me anymore.

"Look, guys. I don't like keeping things from you, but this is none of my business. This is Georgina's thing, and I didn't mean to help her but it happened."

We argued for a bit because they hate it when I keep things from them. Especially when it involved Little Payasa. Eventually they agreed to let it go, but they were still visibly upset with me. Oh well. There was really nothing I could do. I changed the subject to prom—what we were wearing and where we were going to go eat. We decided on a French restaurant (which happens to have delicious pastries) and no limo. At least no limo for me and Martin. And Cindy. We are all on a budget, and I'd rather spend my money on fancy desserts than on a stupid car that is ridiculously way too long.

April 22

Fuck. Fuckity fuck fuck. Ian is the king of all assholes. He told Martin about what happened at his house. Except I am sure he added some things that weren't true and didn't tell the part about where I was like, "Thanks, but no thanks," because after school Martin came to my house just to ask me if it was true and of course I had to tell him what happened. "I can't believe you would do that to me," is all he said before he drove off in his van. And it looked like he had been crying. *Ugh.* Great, I've made a boy cry. I can totally check that off my things-to-do-to-make-sure-your-reputation-of-worst-girlfriend-ever-is-cemented list. I feel bad, but Martin also made me mad because his dumb ass didn't give me a chance to tell him what really happened. Why is life so complicated? Why can't we just kiss who we like when we like? Why are there so many rules? Argh! I hate my life! Insert sounds of sobbing teenage girl here.

HAIKU FOR ROBERT BURNS
Mr. Burns, you were right.
Love is like a red red rose.
Damn those prickly thorns.

Went for a run, but the ice cream I ate afterwards helped a lot more.

April 23

Even though I don't think I'm going to prom anymore, I still had to go pick up the stupid dress from that stupid seamstress.

Sylvia's friend supposedly knows how to make dresses that make you look like a queen. At least that's what Sylvia said. The problem is she lives on the other side of the border, and queens don't live there. Or at least not any queen I want to look like. TJ—the only place those World Vision people ever seem to visit in Mexico. It's not like I don't like Mexico. I love Mexico. One year, when we were doing exceptionally well, and my dad wasn't spending all his money on drugs, we got to go on a family vacation to Guanajuato. It was beautiful. So much history, so much culture, and so much lemon-flavored ice cream made in wooden buckets and sold all over the place. I remember asking my mom if we could live there—but not in this border city, this Tijuana, this U.S.-created hellhole with a fence that cages people in like animals, a visible humiliation that lets the world know who is in charge. This is the first impression people get when they leave the country. And this place is where my prom dress came from. I did not have high hopes to begin with, but later was depressingly more disappointed than I could have ever imagined—my dress a perfect representation of the border.

Lucha—the magical maker of dresses—sewed in a house that smelled of cats and cigarettes. Except there were no cats, and she swore she didn't smoke. She was obviously lying. No house could smell that bad of cigarettes without somebody smoking a least a pack a day. When we showed up to that pigsty of a house, she said the dress wasn't ready.

Sylvia was mad, "¿Para que te pagamos si no iba estar listo?"

Why did we pay her if the dress wasn't going to be ready? Good question. Nothing we could do though, except shop while Lucha put the finishing touches on the dress. We went to El Centro Commercial. Small clothing boutiques, paletearías, lingerie stores, gift shops and lots of places to eat.

Sylvia asked me, "¿Tienes hambre?"

Is the Pope Catholic?

Never ask the fat girl if she is hungry. She's hungry. She's always hungry. Even if she is not, she is, because food is safe and controllable and soothing and salty and sweet, and it doesn't scream at you or make you feel bad unless you are trying on clothes. We ate at Tac's. Like always. Tac's is a tradition whenever we go to Tijuana. Tac's is the only thing I really like about the place. Tacos, huaraches, sopes, tortas, and gorditas. Only the bare essentials are served at Tac's. I got up to the register and placed my usual order, "Un huarache de asada y dos tacos de buche." Eagerly I wait for my fix of dead cow flank and pig esophagus and then it happened...

"Are you sure you want to eat all that?" Buzz kill. Grillman who outweighs me by at least 200 pounds seeks to give me nutritional advice.

"Si." I felt my face fire up.

What else was I supposed to say? "Sorry, Fat Boy, does that seem like too much? Will I be leaving too little for you to eat later?" I ate my huarache and dos tacos de buche in silence. To top off the delightful afternoon, we picked up unmentionables at Mirdyss, a store middle-aged Mexican women swear by. Mirdyss is known for their underwear and bras that lift, tuck, separate, hide, squish, straighten and flatten all that needs lifting, tucking, hiding, squishing, straightening and flattening—as painfully as possible. This is what Sylvia picked out for me: white bra with one-and-a-half inch-straps. Underarm fat pulled in and pushed to front. End result: pointy boobs. Dangerous weapons. If I ever decide to actually wear these medieval torture devices, I'll make sure to wear a sign around my neck that reads: "Beware of Boobs" or "Danger: Impaling May Occur." But I'll just burn it later and save myself from certain injury.

When we got back to Lucha's house, she had finished the dress. I tried it on and it was too tight. It may have been the tacos, or it may have been the huarache, or it may have been the fact that Lucha was the worst seamstress in the world. When she saw it didn't close, she smirked at us and said, "You were in a hurry." I was pissed. Not only did it not fit, but the design was all wrong. I could easily win the world's prettiest piñata contest.

"Pues, es que estas media gordita, mija," Lucha said when she saw my face.

Sylvia stepped in before I shoved a roll of satin down her throat. We were both angry. We left the shack and the stench of cats that didn't exist and cigarettes that were never smoked. Left the country. Back to the U.S. as fast as Sylvia's avocado green Ford could take us.

I wanted a hamburger. Double scoop of coconut pineapple and Rocky Road. Hot Cheetos with lemon and hot sauce. A huge dark chocolate bar. A carne asada taco o torta o las dos cosas. Some beef jerky. Anything. I thought about all the food I would eat later as we drove back, straight past the juggling kids, the fruit vendors, covijas por veinte dólares, the crippled, mangled and poverty-stricken populace quien nos despedía de México lindo y querido.

April 25

I tried to talk to Martin today at school, and he said he needed some time to think about things, that he'd come by my house later today. He should be here at any minute. The more I think about it, the more Martin is getting on my nerves. So maybe I did want Ian to kiss me. But Martin doesn't know that, so why the hell is he so pissed off? He needs to get over it.

Later...

It turns out Ian is a bigger asshole than I thought. He told Martin that I asked if I could go over to his house early because I had something to show him, and then I threw him on the bed and started trying to make out with him. Next time I see him, I will make sure to kick him in the balls. Or at least trip him. Or maybe just tell him off, because who am I kidding? Besides the time I smacked Georgina for saying shit about my dad, I've never hit anyone. I told Martin the truth (well, most of it) and how I told Ian that I wasn't interested and that he got all offended. And then Martin apologized for thinking I would do something like that, that he knew I wasn't like that and that he overreacted. I told him he did totally overreact. But now I am wondering what he meant by *like that*? I am back to feeling guilty because I kind of am *like that*. Oh my God, what is wrong with me?!

April 29

My mom totally surprised me today. After school she asked if I wanted to go to Costco with her, and I was like, "Free samples? I am totally in!" But instead of going to Costco, she took me to the mall to look for a prom dress! She said that Sylvia had told her all about Lucha and Tijuana and the horrible piñata dress and that she had seen that there were some good sales this week at the mall and that maybe we could find something. This was so un-momlike. In fact I was a little anxious—at first. Whenever we have gone shopping together, she ends up making me feel bad about everything I try on, saying it's too tight or "It looks nice, but it would look better if..." It's a bit of a stressful situation shopping with my mom. But I needed a dress, and she seemed to be in a good mood, so I figured it couldn't be that bad. And I was right. We spent the whole afternoon shopping, and I actually found a dress that didn't make me look like I was full of candy, and I looked pretty darn cute if I do say so myself. My mom even said I looked beautiful, which really means a lot to me even though I try to hide it. In the evening, we had dinner at this seafood place. I was so happy we shopped before we ate because I stuffed my face with a whole mojarra frita and some delicious seafood rice. This is the thing about eating with my mom, I am always waiting for the hammer to fall. For the criticisms, for the warnings, for the speeches on diabetes, backaches, high cholesterol and looking good—for the speeches about making sure to look good if you want to find a good husband that I have been hearing since I was like ten and still thought boys were stupid. But today, those speeches were absent. It was nice. I wonder if this is what "normal" mother-daughter relationships are like.

May 2

Time needs to slow down. Prom is in two weeks, and after that it's the senior dinner-dance, and then it's grad night, and then it's graduation. And then that is it—good-bye Ms. Abernard. Good-bye brother who gets on my damn nerves but who I still love with all my heart. And good-bye Pepe's House of Wings. Okay, not really good-bye Pepe's House of Wings because I looked it up, and there is one up north, but I bet it won't have the same look or the same sketchy people (such as man-asking-for-change-with-his-family or my mom's old friend who has gotten too friendly with the bottle but still feels the need to tell me to cut down on my wing consumption) hanging around in the parking lot. Oh, Santa Maria de los Rosales, how I will miss you.

May 3

This would be the part of the movie where I become a bad-ass bitch, like Zoe Saldana, in that movie *Colombiana*, where her thirst for vengeance cannot be satiated until she kills the man responsible for the death of her family—patiently waiting and destroying everything he loves until she gets to his sorry, disgusting ass.

Sometimes, everything seems like a movie to me. Like we are somehow detached from a reality that happens outside of our city limits. Earlier this year there was a story on the news about a girl who had gotten drunk at a party, like totally shit-faced drunk. Semi-typical teenage thing, I guess, though I don't do that. But I know a lot of people who do. This girl was then raped by several members of the football team who texted pictures to their friends and posted about it. This is not a semi-typical teenage thing to do. At all. But this happened far away, so I thought things like this only happen far away. Things like that don't happen in Santa Maria—sure we have major drug problems, poverty, burglary issues and the occasional visit from the dumb-ass Neo-Nazis from Stupidville about twenty miles away. But those idiots (usually) only make their visits to the Home Depot where the day laborers are waiting to get picked up to go to work. So we have those kinds of problems here. But rape, I never hear about rape. So I stupidly, and happily, assumed that that was one crime that we could be proud to say didn't happen in our city. But I was 300% wrong about that.

German raped Cindy. She told us tonight when we were over at her place just hanging out and talking about prom and joking about people having sex in their parents' back seat, and I made some dumb comment about her and German, and she started crying. I was like *Oh shit, I crossed the line again*. And that's when she told us what really happened that night. She said she was a little drunk when German and her started making out in the car, and he started pulling up her dress, and she was all for it at first, but then she changed her mind, and he said that she had already said yes, and she couldn't say no and that was that. She said he didn't hit her or treat her badly, but he held her down, and she cried the whole time. I didn't know what to say. And neither did Sebastian. I mean what can you say to your friend who just finished telling you she was raped? There is no Hallmark card for that. And the *I'm sorrys* we sputtered sounded ridiculously unfitting for such an occasion. We just hugged her and tried to convince her to call the police, but she said there was no point. He didn't beat her or anything, and no one would believe her.

The whole way home I just kept thinking about what I've heard all my life from my mom and other women whenever boys have done something stupid and/or wrong: "Boys will be boys," and what a load of bullshit that is. I had to write about it.

INSTRUCTIONS FOR UNDERSTANDING WHAT *BOYS WILL BE BOYS* REALLY MEANS

1. You're wearing that little dress tonight? Remember, boys will be boys, so be careful.
2. If you drink way too much, your body is fair game—for anyone or anyones. Boys will be boys, and you just made it easier.

3. When a girl says no, you might want to consider your position. I don't think she meant yes. But I'm a girl, so what do I know? But because boys will be boys, you don't really have to think about it.

4. If she is crying, that is definitely a sign that she means no. But since you are an asshole, you won't give it a second thought, so proceed. She was wearing that little dress (remember?), and boys will be boys, after all. That's what our parents say.

5. It's not rape if she said yes first. Everyone knows that. She's your girlfriend and obviously she knows that boys will be boys, otherwise she wouldn't have teased you.

6. Because boys will be boys, he's not going to use a condom (he likes the real deal), so you might just get pregnant. But hopefully, you won't get AIDS or herpes or chlamydia. So you should feel good about that. Besides, babies are cute.

7. If he doesn't beat you up, then it's not really rape. Everyone knows that too. Also, he wasn't a stranger. He was someone you cared about, just a boy being a boy.

8. Remember how your mother warned you that boys only want one thing from you? Well, it's not your straight A's or your excellent drawing skills or your extensive knowledge of action films. It's the thing you have guarded (hint: it's between your legs) your whole life from everyone: your cousin who came to stay for two weeks, your strange uncle Tony, that teacher in the 2nd grade—they were all just boys being boys.

9. It's your fault. Even if you're disabled, old or young. You should know better.
10. Boys will be boys.

May 5

Cinco de Mayo! Woo! Another holiday where people get to use sombreros and fake mustaches as proof of their understanding and commitment to learning about my heritage. I mean, I love fake mustaches as much as anyone—they're pretty hilarious—but I don't think I've seen a Mexican in a handlebar mustache since Emiliano Zapata. The last person I saw who wore a sombrero in his day-to-day life was my abuelito Isauro, and he was super old, and he is now super dead. Not that we don't wear them—we do. But, come on. There has to be more to us than that. Between all those mustaches and sombreros and wanting to kill German for what he did for Cindy and worrying about prom, I'm ready to give up on life. Not really, but I do need to pass my Algebra II class or Berkeley will ask me to stay the hell out because they don't let people step foot on their campus who don't know how to do quadratic equations. I think part of why I can't concentrate on stupid math is that my mom is totally guilting me about even thinking about leaving. Mexican moms are so good at the whole guilt trip thing. It's like they're required to take a class in it before they gave birth. She says she needs me around. "What if your tía Bertha gets tired of staying here? Or she finds a boyfriend?" I tell her, "The day that tía Bertha gets a boyfriend is the day I give up Hot Cheetos. It's not going to happen." Then she pulls out the big guns: the what-good-girls-do and what-bad-girls-do card. She will forever think of me as bad when I leave. I know that. Like I did it on purpose to hurt her. And I can't help but wonder if that in fact will make me a bad daughter? She says that only White girls take off like that because they don't care about leaving their families. "A las gabachillas les gusta andar de locas, por eso se van de sus casas." This is her response whenever I mention moving away. I don't think that White girls move away because they want to abandon their families and want to be free to have wild monkey sex whenever they please. In fact, I am 100% certain that Mexican girls like having wild monkey sex too. Actually, I think that having wild monkey sex may be on the mind of many teenage girls. Hormones— and things like hate and love—know no boundaries when it comes to race and gender. I think that all we want is to be free. I also worry that college will be too hard. What if I don't make it? What if everyone is smarter than me, and I don't know what the professors are talking about? What if this fat girl doesn't have what it takes in college, and all of a sudden I'm covered in pig's blood because my mom was right, and all they do is laugh at me? *Okay, Gabi, chill.* Things I need to cut down on:

1. Beef jerky after midnight.
2. Stephen King novels that involve controlling mothers and buckets of pig's blood.

May 6

Took an Algebra II practice quiz today and did alright. Next Friday is another quiz. It's our last chapter test before our final exam. If I can keep doing this well, I will have no problem passing the class. This is definitely due to all the time Sebastian has spent tutoring me. It's been worth having to hear all about his stupid boyfriend and all their screwing around. To be honest, I have been a little jealous. I've been wondering if Martin and I will have sex sometime. How would that be? I don't think I want him to see me naked, I mean, *eww gross*. Sometimes I don't want to see myself naked. Sometimes the mirror is my enemy. I mean, I would never dare ask it who the fairest of them all is because I know the response would make me weep. But sometimes I feel okay about how I look and even think, *I'd tap that, why not?*

Maybe it will be like the movies. Cut to Gabi's first time: "Something" by the Beatles playing softly in the background of a dim candlelit room, with a huge heart-shaped bed and chilled sparkling cider (that's what it would have to be since neither of us drink, but both of us like apple cider). Martin would hold my hand, and we'd jump on the bed and go under the covers only to resurface moments later, content and satisfied. But how long, I don't know. Ten minutes? Twenty minutes? An hour? How long does it really last? I mean, I know movies have to do major editing due to time constraints. This is something I have to look up. Now that I think about it, I think I saw the heart-shaped bed in a Muppet's movie or something. Great—how I imagine my first time stems from Miss Piggy's (a muppet's!) life. *SMH*. I am so over-thinking this. That's my problem. I think about these things way too much. But these very important issues were never addressed in sex ed. And it wasn't like we could ask the teacher—that would have been totally embarrassing. I feel like Margaret in Judy Blume's *Are You There God, It's Me Margaret*? Except instead of waiting for my period, I am waiting for my first time to see a boy naked. I wonder if this is normal? Probably not good in any case. Argh!!! *FML*. Seriously.

On a totally unsex-related note, Ms. Abernard has asked us to bring our best five poems from the year on Monday. The class will finally be putting together *Black Cloud* (our anthology), and then we will be having a reading where the whole school will have the option to attend. Most folks won't go (I imagine), but some will (she even invited the superintendent!), so I want to be ready. Martin is coming over this weekend, and we are going to go over poems and choosing which ones we should turn in and which ones we should leave out. I guess that wasn't as unsex- related as I hoped.

May 7

My mom asked me to invite Martin for breakfast this morning for chilaquiles. She seems to really like him, or maybe she's happy that there is at least one candidate for my hand in marriage. He came over, and we all had breakfast together: Mom, Beto, tía Bertha, Ernie, Martin and me. It felt good to be surrounded by people you love and who love you—like after all the crap we've been through this year, things are finally looking up. I don't want to get too comfortable though because it's just like us to be feeling good when all of a sudden massive amounts of shit fall into our laps, and it's time for major clean up.

After breakfast, Martin and I started searching through poems, but we got so caught up in poetry that suddenly it was 5:30. Martin was supposed to be home like an hour before that. Luckily, his dad won't flip out as long as he calls and tells him where he is at. Part of it is because his dad is way more mellow than my mom, and the other part is probably because he is a boy. This is part of the "boys will be boys" mantra that we live by. Like my brother doesn't have the same rules I do even though I'm older and obviously more responsible (and mature). For example: the other day he was going to go out with this girl and my mom didn't even ask to meet her, all she said was, "Make sure you take a condom with you."

When I started dating Eric, she wanted to meet his parents right away (I had to beg her to not do that because it wasn't like we were planning a wedding or anything). Before I could go out with Martin (on a real date), he had to come over and meet her. "So if something happens to you, I know how to describe him to the police," was her response when I asked her why. But my brother is going out with some girl (she could easily be a serial killer, a fugitive, forty years old—or twelve years old for all we know) and all she says is, "Make sure you take a condom with you?" Really, Mom, what the hell is that all about? Obviously, I didn't say that out loud because I'm no dummy, but I sure did think it. Although I was going to call her out on her hypocrisy, I figured there was no point. She was only going to say, "It's different. Beto is a boy, and they can't help it. Besides, you have more to lose than him." So I just kept my mouth shut.

By the time Martin had to leave, we had picked our poems for Monday. It feels good to be prepared with at least one assignment finished ahead of time. Now for my English essay on *Beowulf*, my letter to my senator for government and homework for Algebra II. So much to do. I don't know how Cindy does it with the baby.

May 9

Good day at school. Had yogurt with Sebastian and his boyfriend and then got home. Turns out my essay on *Beowulf* wasn't due until Thursday, which means I am ahead of schedule (for the first time in my entire school career). So now I have some extra time to do other things, like write a poem about love. Usually I hate love poems—they're corny and flowery and so blah. But Martin's been giving me some to get me to change my mind about them. He gave me the Robert Burns poem, and he gave me a few sonnets by William Shakespeare, but so far my favorite love poem has been by Pablo Neruda, "Tonight I Can Write." There's something about the poem that is so sad but so romantic, and I think I know how Pablo felt when he wrote it. I was so moved by the poem, I thought I would write one for Martin.

LOVE POEM INSPIRED BY MARTIN (AND ROBERT BURNS)
Do not forget about the thorns on the roses
when you say that love is like a red red rose.
Why can't it be like a white rose?
Or a pink rose?
Or a yellow rose?
Roses are so hard to get to,
so hard to pick.
You have to use gloves

or risk
your skin
to get at them.
Is that what you meant, Mr. Burns?
That because roses are so hard to get at
that love must be like a rose.

What about geraniums?

Love is like a white geranium.
It grows like a weed
overpowering the ground—
if you don't take care of it
prune it
shape it
it climbs walls
and hides
insects
that slowly eat at it
making it die.
Easily grown
and easily withered.

Yes, Mr. Burns, I think love is like a stubborn geranium.

Not very Pablo Neruda-like, but it's how I feel.

May 11

P-Day is almost here. Prom. I didn't think I'd be this excited about it, but I am. I don't even know why—I mean, I know why, but still. Cindy and I have make-up appointments at the mall and for hair we are going to my neighbor who said she would charge us cheap. Okay, I'm lying to myself—I know exactly why I am getting all nervous and excited. Things have been getting extremely serious with Martin. Like really serious and hot and heavy. What if we go all the way at prom? I know I need to be ready. I need some sort of anti-pregnancy plan. Obviously, I am not taking birth control. My mom would flip, and I'd probably get kicked out. I've heard some girls talk about "pulling out," but that seems risky and messy from what I've read online. And how do you even ask someone to do that? *Ew.* So that leaves condoms. But shouldn't he buy those on his own? I know I'd be too embarrassed to buy them. But what if I did? And what if he doesn't even want to have sex with me, and here I am with a box of condoms and...I can't even think about that. I am pretty sure he wants to though. A few weeks ago we were making out, and he actually felt my boob for the first time, and I was a little shocked, but I tried not to let it show. It got a little awkward because he asked if it was okay. I mean I was totally into it, so obviously it was okay. The more I thought about it, the more I'm glad he asked and didn't just assume. I kind of wanted him to go further than he was going, but I didn't

say anything because I thought that I would have seemed way too slutty.

Right? It's hard enough to have those thoughts in my own head, away from

the public, keeping everyone safe, because girls are not supposed to think

that way. But then, as if by magic, my doubt of whether or not my thoughts

were normal was put to rest. Today in Algebra II, boys were joking about

jacking off (which was really making me uncomfortable because as much as

I think about sex stuff in my mind, I don't really want to talk about it with

everyone, but I didn't know how to tell them to shut up without sounding

lame, so I didn't). What the boys were really trying to do was gross us out,

and it was kind of working. Finally, Debby Allan (one of the students with

the highest grades in the class) got tired of them and said, "Well, don't

feel so special, everyone does that. Girls just don't admit it because if we

did people would think we're sluts instead of normal human beings." And

then she looked at me and said, "Right, Gabi?" I could feel my face turn red

as I said very quietly, "I don't," and turned back to my assignment. Either

way my answer proved her point. Still, I don't feel comfortable talking

about things like that in public. I don't think sex is bad, but I'm not about

to admit how much I want to have sex with Martin. I'm not about to tell

everyone, "Hey, guess what, guys? My boyfriend grabbed my boob, and I

liked it! If he tries to get a little further next time, I am soooo gonna let him! How about that? Stay tuned for the next edition of *The Adventures of Gabi's Vagina*, now in 3D and IMAX!" Yeah, that's not gonna happen.

May 13

High five me! Another A on my math quiz! Sebastian is truly a math genius and a life saver.

After school I did something either stupid or smart. Not sure yet. I finally decided that if there was any possibility of Martin and me having sex, I had to be safe and went out and bought condoms. I didn't tell Cindy because she would be mad at me, and I would probably get a whole lecture on why sex is bad. She still thinks that what German did was her fault and that that's how boys are. I've tried to tell her that Martin is not like that at all, and she's like, "That's what you think." So I just stay away from that subject. Sebastian, on the other hand, would probably want to give me tips, and that would be kind of weird as I don't think it works the same way for both of us. The only person I could trust in this situation would be Georgina, and I haven't really held a conversation with her since after she solved her problem. I went to the Stuffix Pharmacy right after school and prayed it would be empty. And it was. Georgina was the only person working, and she had just gotten there.

"What? Don't tell me you need a pregnancy test too? That'd be three in a row for our class." She was joking but looked worried at the same time.

"No! Of course not. But look...I need...well...I want..." I didn't even know how to say it.

I was in total lobster mode at this point, and she just started laughing, "What? Do you have a yeast infection?"

"Ewww! Gross! Isn't that something that old ladies get? No. I...never mind."

I was just about to turn around when she said, "Oh my God, are you looking for condoms?"

"What?"

"You want Aisle Three."

"What?"

"¿Estas sorda? Aisle Three." She spoke louder and more slowly.

I walked over to Aisle Three and sure enough, there were the rubber gods in all their splendor—the thin veil of latex that would seemingly protect my unfertilized eggs from Martin's fertilizing crazed sperm. They were flavored, textured, magnum (whatever that meant—perhaps offering maximum strength) and came in various bright neon colors. My mind raced: Why would I want flavored condoms? I am so not putting anything that would go in a condom in my mouth. *Gross.* And I didn't know there were different sizes! *Ugh*. I thought this was a one-size-fits-all situation. But alas, this poor ignorant maiden was confronted with too many choices. It was like my first time at Del Taco all over again: everything had its potential upsides, but everything also had the potential to be a horribly gut-wrenching mistake.

I was just about to give up and walk away when another customer walked in with a crying baby. As I turned and looked her way, the pregnancy tests next to the condoms caught my eye and forced me to confront the consequences of being a big wuss and not buying the condoms. If I wasn't prepared for a potential sexual rendezvous on prom night—or any other night for that matter—I could be in the same boat as Cindy or Georgina or my mom. And that is not anywhere near where I want to be at this moment in my life. I want to go to college. I want to be free. I want to move out of this one-horse town. *Gabi*, I said to myself, *you do not need a baby in your life*. I sucked it up, grabbed a medium and hoped for the best. Driving home, sweaty and red-faced, all I thought about was where I would hide my new companions and about the Milano cookies under my bed that I was about to devour. Oddly enough, I was also in the mood for some Del Taco.

May 14

Holy shit. Yup. That's the kind of morning I'm having. Yesterday I was so stressed about not knowing what size condoms to buy at the pharmacy that I zoned out. In fact, I zoned out so much that I didn't notice that after (or maybe before?) the arrival of the customer with the crying baby, my tía Bertha had walked into the pharmacy and had seen me make my purchase. She didn't say anything when I got home last night, but this morning, when I was taking out the trash, she cornered me in the back yard.

"Buenos dias, Gabi."

"Good morning, tía."

Awkward silence.

"So you have a big night tonight, ¿verdad? Lots of fun and dancing with your little boyfriend."

"Yup."

The whole time she's giving me this weird look that's making me real uncomfortable. And I can feel that some sort of storm is coming, but I don't know when or what kind.

And then it hits. And I realize that it is a major Level Five shitstorm.

"I saw you at the farmacia yesterday."

Fuuuuuuuuuuuuuuuck, I think, *I'm dead*. She's going to tell my mom and after the, "See, that's why I don't want you hanging out with Cindy! You want to go to college to be like some easy gabacha, and you've starting practicing now!" tirade, she will take me out back and sacrifice me to an ancient god and pray I am reincarnated as a good daughter or a goldfish. At the least, I will be forbidden to leave the house and definitely not allowed to move out. But I try to play dumb. Maybe my tía had just seen me walk out of the pharmacy and didn't even notice my purchase.

"Wh...huh?"

"I saw what you were buying too. Little globitos."

Balloons. She saw me buying the freaking balloons.

"Oh...those weren't for me, tía." Technically that was not a lie.

"Don't worry, I'm not going to tell your mom. That's your business. I admire that you are being careful and protecting yourself. Very smart. I wish I would have thought of that when I was young, and I wouldn't have gotten...anyway I'm not telling your mom. But I want you to remember that God will know. He will know what you did...or what you do. He knows every sin you commit, and he will be watching you. I want you to be thinking about that tonight before you do any cochinadas that might condemn you to Hell. Because you don't want to go to Hell, mi'ja. Do you?"

She came towards me with her hand extended, and I flinched. But she just patted my shoulder. She walked away and left me out there shocked and contemplating what it was she had "gotten" and about how God may be watching me have sex tonight and how creepy that thought was and how I pray to God she won't tell my mom—otherwise this may be my last journal entry.

May 15

Oh my God! It is 4:30 a.m. I just got yelled at for coming in two hours later than I was supposed to, even though I called. But it doesn't matter, it was worth the yelling.

Prom was so much fun! Martin picked me up on time. After dinner we got to the train station (this year's theme seemed to be a mix of barnyard fun and alien adventure). We danced all night long to every kind of music the DJ played. I didn't even know Martin could dance. Afterwards, we were all going to eat but decided not to because I was really afraid of breaking curfew. Martin dropped Cindy off and then was going to drop me off, but we still had some time before I had to get home so we drove around talking about school, college, poetry and a bunch of other things. It turned out that there was no one at his house this weekend because his dad had taken off to Tijuana for a baptism. I was feeling daring and asked Martin if we could go to his house. His eyes got a little big, and I could tell he was getting nervous and that made it more exciting.

"Um...yeah. But there isn't anyone home so it'd just be us."

"I know."

"Oh."

I didn't really know what was going to happen. Maybe we would just make out. Maybe we would go all the way. Maybe we would just read poems. But something was going to happen. When we got to his house, he turned on one of the lamps in the living room. We sat on the couch for a bit and talked. Then he leaned in to kiss me. At that moment I wasn't too fat, I wasn't too white, I wasn't bad, I was just me. He asked if I was sure it was okay, and I said yes and we went from there. My brain forgot all about the negatives and let the lower half of my body take control of what was happening. I was nervous. I immediately realized that it was not like the movies at all. There was no way you could get things done under sheets, and there was no easy smooth way to take off your clothes. Buttons take time. And while we struggled with clothes, I couldn't stop thinking about what my tía Bertha had said about God looking down on us. Was he watching right now? And would I get sent to Hell? Was I behaving like some sex-crazed White girl like my mom was worried about? Did race have anything to do with the fact that all I wanted was to take Martin's pants off, but his shoes were getting in the way? I didn't know, and I soon forgot about all that.

Afterwards I realized that it didn't seem as satisfying (it hurt at first—not I'm-going-to-die pain, but it was not Rocky-Road-ice-cream either) as it does in the movies, and it was a lot messier than I would ever have imagined. Damn you, Hollywood! I'm sure this was because it was our first time. I hope it was because it was our first time. Martin held me for a while in his arms, and it was the best feeling ever. But then it turned to the worst feeling ever when we realized that it was super late, and I was like, "Oh shit. My mom is going to kill me!"

He drove me home and walked me to my door. My mom was there. After she got done yelling at him for not bringing me back on time and after he left, she let me have it.

"¡Quien sabe en donde andabas! I was worried! You said ten minutes and that was forty-five minutes ago! ¡No vas a salir toda esta semana y no telefono! No phone! None. And don't even think about asking to go out this week or weekend. Don't even think about it."

I didn't even argue back. I was feeling content. Am I a bad girl because I don't feel that guilty? Probably. But the thing is, I am starting to care less about that badness.

I had to write this down. Can't stop thinking about what just happened and thinking about what Martin may be thinking about. I left the unopened box of condoms in my tía Bertha's purse with a note that read, "Didn't need them after all."

Martin had been prepared.

May 16

Tía Bertha hugged me this morning and said that she was so proud of me and that God is proud of me too. That she had prayed that I would make the right choice and that this was proof that God really listened to her. I just smiled and nodded my head. I hurried and left for school. I didn't tell Cindy or Sebastian about what had happened between me and Martin, and I'm not sure if I want to. I don't want the lecture that is sure to follow. Cindy will be mad. Sebastian will probably want all the details, and I don't think I want to share anything with him because even if it did feel kind of good, part of me wonders if we did it right. I mean it was my first time, and there is no handbook, which means I could have technically been doing it wrong and would have no freaking clue. Plus, there are things I want to keep private. Also, since I hadn't talked to Martin since it happened (because I'm grounded), I didn't know how he was feeling. I was worried that it would be really awkward because now that my hormones aren't all over the place, I realized that he saw me NAKED! OMG! Another person has seen me naked. What if he was like, *Oh gross! I didn't know this is what was under the hood!* What if he regretted it? I was so worried and mad at myself at the same time (because why am I so worried about what others think about how I look?) that I was giving myself a headache. When I finally got to school and found my comrades, I saw that Martin had bought me some flowers and a card (an after-sex card? Was I supposed to get him one? There should really be a handbook.) Inside the card read:

"Gabi, I love you."

And then the bastard rewrote Shakespeare's Sonnet 130. He is so freaking cheesy.

> My mistress' eyes are everything like the sun;
> Coral is pale compared to how her lips are red;
> If snow be white, why then her breasts are snow;
> If others hairs be wires, upon her head soft brown filament.
> I have seen roses damasked, red and white,
> And brighter roses see I in her cheeks;
> And in no perfumes is there more delight
> Than in the breath that of my mistress when she speaks.
> I love to hear her speak, and well I know
> That no music hath more a pleasing sound;
> I grant I never saw a goddess go;
> My mistress when she glides her feet just touch the ground.
> And, by heaven, I know my love more rare
> As any she belied with false compare.

May 19

My moments of bliss have ended. I thought teachers would be laying off the work because we are graduating, but they're not. We have another essay due in English, a chapter to outline in government, math homework, physics, Spanish—and let's not forget all about the reading for our poetry anthology tomorrow.

Head is spinning. I feel like I'm going to throw up.

May 20

Ms. Abernard did a really good job with the anthology. The first-ever issue of *Black Cloud Review* was full of awesome poetry from our class—and also art and photographs from Mr. Taylor's classes. We got to pick the art pieces that went in it. Of course, I had to pick some of Sebastian's art. One was a landscape drawing of Skyline, and the other was a photograph of two guys holding hands. There was a lot of argument over that photograph.

Clementino Noriega had said, "I don't want no fucking picture of two fags in the magazine. That's stupid. Why do we have to do whatever gays tell us to do?"

First off: Clementino is an idiot. Secondly: When do gay people tell us to do things? When? When they ask for equal rights? That's not so much telling us to do things as sticking to the promise of everyone is created equal. I had never seen Ms. Abernard so pissed. She's usually really laid back, but Clementino's stupidity brought out the monster within, I guess. She didn't yell at him, but she sure did put him in his place, telling him that if all he had to add to our anthology was ignorance and hate, then perhaps his voice and opinions were not needed or desired. Then she wrote him a referral for using foul language, and I heard her mutter under her breath (because I was sitting right next to her desk when this all went down), "...and if I could give him one for being a fucking idiot, I'd do that too." I don't know if anyone else heard her, but if they did, no one said anything. I so did not realize that teachers cussed or that they didn't like some of their students. At that moment, Ms. Abernard became my new hero.

There were so many people at the reading: administrators, teachers, students—and our parents. Ms. Abernard had invited our families without telling us. For some of us, this was too much. A few students said that they wouldn't be able to read out loud because they didn't want their families to hear them. It was hard enough to read in front of strangers but to read in front of our families was brutal. I bit the bullet and read my dad poem, my grandpa poem, and the love poem I had written after reading Robert Burns and Pablo Neruda. I was afraid my mom was going to get mad and say something about putting our family business out there, but she surprised me and said she was proud. After the reading, we all signed each other's books and Ms. Abernard's, who swore that we would all be famous writers one day (I think teachers are required to say things like that). And after, we got to eat the snacks that our parents had brought (my mom brought conchitas) and coffee. I felt almost adultlike. Until my mom totally killed it and made me feel like the dumb teenager that I am.

She finally got to meet Martin's dad, and they hit it off. Not in a romantic way, but in a Mexican-parent-who-is-from-the-same-place-in-Mexico-and-is-also-a-widow/er kind of way. They both started talking about their dreams for us and how they wished we didn't have to move so far and blah blah blah. And then they (my mom) did what every parent does—said something uncomfortable to embarrass their child.

My mom said, "Well, I'm just glad that Gabi is waiting to have sex until she is married and that Martin is being a respectful young man."

Why, Mom? Why does she think this is appropriate or necessary? Who does that? It's like she's trying to prove that I have unused goods—still in their original wrapper—just in case anyone is interested in marriage. I'm surprised she doesn't add the fact that I also have a goat as part of my dowry. She might as well open my mouth and let the buyers inspect my teeth. I wanted to crawl in a hole and die. Instead I just shoved an oatmeal raisin cookie in my face and tried to act like I didn't hear her.

Though—if anyone looked at my face, which was sure to be a beautiful shade of crimson—it would have been obvious that something bad had just occurred.

Martin's dad looked over at us (uncomfortably), smiled and said, "Pues si verdad. Of course."

He knew. Martin's dad knew what had happened. He knew what my mom didn't know: that my goods were used and could not be returned to the manufacturer. I almost died. I looked at Martin who looked at me with a panicked smile and beads of sweat forming on his forehead. We both walked away from that conversation and had a few more cookies.

So, except for my mom putting my sex life on blast with my boyfriend's dad, it was a great night.

May 23

I am no longer grounded and am going to celebrate by hanging out at Cindy's house in about an hour. Graduation is in three freaking weeks! The year has gone by so fast. Seniors take finals this week so we know whether or not we graduate. That would be so shitty to find out this week that you won't be graduating. But since Sebastian has been on my ass about Algebra II, I have no doubt that I am Berkeley-bound.

I hadn't seen Martin since Friday. We went off campus for lunch (I hadn't used my off campus pass since we took Georgina to the clinic), and I asked him if he had told his dad about us—it has been eating away at me all weekend.

"Yes. I told him."

"Why would you do that? Now your dad is going to think I'm a slut or something."

I was mortified and felt like crying. Tears were about to burst.

"Why would he? I don't think you are. I told my dad partly because I tell him everything...and mostly because he found my condoms in my pants when he was doing laundry."

"What?"

"He just said that he didn't want me having sex because I wasn't ready for the responsibility that came with it. But that he knew he couldn't stop me and that he was happy that at least I was trying to be responsible. He also said that I have to respect you and not pressure you to do things you don't want to do, and if you say no, it's no."

"Are you serious?" I couldn't believe that an adult would say something like that. My mom certainly wouldn't have said something like that.

"Yeah. He hates all that macho *boys will be boys* bullshit. He says it's an excuse for men to act like animals. And I totally agree with him."

"That is so not how my mom thinks. And he was much cooler about it than my aunt who caught me buying condoms and said that I would go to Hell if we had sex."

He smiled at that.

"Well, it's a good thing I don't believe in Hell."

I was totally caught off guard with that one. I had never met an atheist.

"Wait. What? You don't believe in God?"

"I don't know if I do. I have my doubts. But if there is a God, I'm not sure that his main purpose is to send two people who love each other to Hell for having sex. There are worse things in life and bigger fish he should be frying."

"Hmmm. I had never really thought of it that way. I know that I have my questions about how we believe in God—like why aren't there female priests? Why is birth control bad? Is it really a bad idea for priests to marry and have children? Or who decides how we should interpret the "word of God"?—but there isn't anyone I have ever trusted enough to talk with about them. My mom would freak out and even Cindy and Sebastian would think I was weird."

"No judgement here, Gabi. None. I love the person you are and wouldn't want you to pretend to be something you're not—whether that means having the faith of a mustard seed or trying to find your faith."

That guy makes me so hot. I am so in love with him.

May 24

Every time I see German the urge to hurt him—sincerely hurt him—grows. And today I had my chance. I saw him, arm around some poor girl's shoulder (she couldn't have been more than a freshman) and couldn't help but wonder if he would do the same to her as he did to Cindy. If he did, would she be the one to stop him? Could she find her voice in order to silence his? This is the thing with me: as soon as I start thinking about something, I can't let it go. It's exhausting. I wish I could just turn my brain off and let it take a small vacation—near the beach, drinking lemonade and eating pizza. But I can't. After Cindy told me about German, everywhere I looked, wherever there were couples or pregnant teens, I would wonder if it was consensual. Because of our idea of how good girls behave and how bad girls behave, many girls are too afraid or ashamed to speak up. Afraid of what everyone would say about them, afraid of being called liars, sluts or ofrecidas. This is what Cindy and Georgina (and my mom) have taught me. So, when I saw German today, I was consumed with anger that had been simmering for almost a month, and suddenly it was a roaring boil. I tried to stop myself. Tried to remind myself that I had promised Cindy that I wouldn't say anything to anyone, especially not to German. It wasn't my place to ask for justice (okay, maybe I felt like it was my place because someone had to stop him, and I knew that

Cindy wasn't going to do anything. Was I supposed to let some guy keep on treating girls like they were his own personal playground? That's not how I function. But I KNOW I should've kept my mouth shut. It wasn't my place.)

This is the thing about German. He's hot. Like super hot. He's got silky caramel skin, the best hair ever, dimples, a body that won't quit (he's on the soccer team and I've watched them practice—shirtless), an awesome sense of style (the boy could be a fashion model), a decent grade point average, and (the biggest tool in his arsenal) he's a smooth talker. I'm surprised he doesn't spit honey every time he speaks. Freshman year, I had a secret crush on him. No one knows about this, and it's a secret I'll take to my grave. Obviously, I can totally see why girls would flock to him. But after realizing the true extent of his scumbag ways, he seems dirty, like he doesn't shower or oozes a foul stench whenever he walks—like some insect warding off birds with its poisonous nature.

So there he was with his greasy, stinky paws all over this poor girl when he noticed me walking towards them. German nodded at me and sent one of his most charming smiles my way. For a second, I was almost like, "Could he really ever rape someone? I mean, look at those big eyes! He's too hot to force someone to sleep with him." Then I almost slapped myself across the face for being such an idiot. Cindy wouldn't have made it up. To think that he wouldn't have raped someone because he was hot was insane and stupid. Of course he did it. It was probably much easier because people wouldn't believe that he would "have to" rape someone. People would assume that they were lucky to have slept with him. I came to my senses and flipped him off. Why would he even think I wanted to say hi to him? He raped my best friend. Though he probably didn't know that I knew that, so he assumed that this bird couldn't smell the noxious gasses. I wonder if he even knows that it was rape, or does he think that's how it's supposed to go down, with a girl crying the whole time?

He looked taken aback, and he shouted at me, "Fuck you too, stupid gorda!"

And I responded with a, "Oh no! You couldn't fuck me, German. Not with that small of a package. And didn't I hear that you had some sort of herpes or something that you can only get from having sex with livestock?" Comebacks are not my strongest weapon.

He got so mad that he shoved the girl aside and came at me like he was going to hit me. I stood my ground as he put his face up to mine, breathing his nasty ass breath over my lips.

"You better shut your fucking mouth, bitch. Or else—"

"Or else what, German," I growled at him. "Are you going to rape me like you did Cindy? You fucking asshole! Wannabe player! You ain't gonna do shit to me!"

He was totally caught off guard with that. By the look on his face, he obviously didn't think she had said anything. He probably hoped that she would never say anything. I imagine that's how rapists think.

"Yeah, I know what you did."

"Your stupid friend doesn't know what she's talking about," he stammered. He was nervous which led me to believe that he knew what he did was wrong. But he couldn't keep his trap shut, "Rape? Pfft. She wanted it. How could she not? All girls want this." He backed up and opened his arms as if showing off his body. "And your friend, she was begging for it."

The levee broke. I hurricane. I flood. I baptismal waters. God the punisher. Ancient being full of wrath. Hammer of Thor. Bolt of Zeus. Huitzilopochtli emerging from Coatepec—recently birthed and thirsty for vengeance. Chola from the barrio that I could never be. I was pissed. German, German, German: his name echoing in my head, begging me to strike him.

I would like to write that I pummeled him. That I was a teenage girl possessed, and there was nothing left of German but pits of skin and bone, clinging from the biology building at Santa Maria de los Rosales High School. That I had sent him to Hell where he belongs. Or (perhaps a little less violent) that suddenly I became some incredibly vicious (and talented) fighting animal. That my skills surprised everyone, and I found my true calling as an MMA fighter or world-famous championship boxer rather than an English geek. But alas, Journal, I cannot lie to you. This is the only place I can be the most myself and I have to be honest.

What really happened was this: I was furious. How dare he say that my friend was begging for it? I kneed him in the crotch and pushed him to the ground and (because I've never been in a fight before and don't know proper fighting etiquette or procedure) I straddled him and kept him down with my weight—the first time in my life that being overweight came in handy. Maybe this was the reason I hadn't lost weight. God had a plan for me all along! And that plan was to overpower one of the hottest guys in school and slap the shit out of him for raping my best friend while his girlfriend watched in horror and tried to pull me off. I don't think God works that way, if he/she is out there. But if I were to believe there was a "plan," this would definitely have to be a part of it. If only for humor, if for nothing else.

I don't know how long I was on top of German slapping him around. I do know that eventually I was pulled off by security. My mother was called and charges were pressed

May 25

I was suspended from school for a week which means that I can kiss my admission to Berkeley good-bye. I've been crying in bed all morning, my pillow is the wettest it's ever been—super gross. At the time, slapping the shit out of German felt like it was a good idea. Like the only thing I could do. But now...I'm sure there were better options. Cindy was so pissed when she found out, and I don't blame her. She called me after school yesterday, and I had to come clean. It didn't feel right to lie to her about this. She started crying and said, "Why couldn't you just let it go? It wasn't any of your business!" I was crying too, but how could I tell her that I didn't think it was fair that he got away with what he did and that he could do the same thing to other girls. But she's right, it wasn't my place. It wasn't my choice to make, no matter if it seemed or felt like the right thing to do. Obviously, German didn't tell anyone the real reason why I attacked him. He just said that I was a crazy bitch, and—because he has no record of violent behavior or behavior issues at all—they believed him. I don't have a violent record either, but since I was the one who was doing the slapping, I was the one who was suspended. The principal got super angry with my answer to her question, "Why did you hurt German? Did he hurt you?" Maybe she expected me to say, "He broke my heart, or I saw him push someone, or I was angry because he wouldn't date me," or some more understandable explanation, but all I said was, "Because assholes deserve that and more." I don't even remember saying that really, but I guess I must have—it was on the form they sent home with my mom. Speaking of which, she's super pissed. And super disappointed. I don't know which is worse. She said that she never expected me to act like that. But what really got her upset was the fact that I wouldn't tell her why I lashed out against German. I am grounded for the next few weeks and won't be able to go to grad night, and the principal is debating whether or not I will be able to walk on graduation day. *Yay me.*

May 26

Day Two in Alcatraz: the other inmates seem to be of the criminally insane variety, especially the one they call "Bertha." I have observed her leaving her cell to feed a small child she has taken under her wing. This all seems normal. However, yesterday I observed a small red truck pull up outside the penitentiary walls and "Bertha" walked out, looked around, making sure the coast was clear before approaching the vehicle. The coast was clear (sort of, because I was snooping out of my window) and so she leaned in and gave the driver a kiss. Maybe staying home this week will be worth it in chisme.

Tía Bertha was actually very vocal about my little tussle. "Good girls never behave that way, Gabi. Never. You were lucky that Martin was interested in you in the first place, but now with this? Ha! No me llamo Bertha Hernandez if he comes around again."

I couldn't help myself and smiled back at her, "Do good girls also kiss strange men who pull up to their house in red pickup trucks in the middle of the morning?"

Tía Bertha's eyes got huge. And her jaw dropped. She was sooo not expecting that. I probably shouldn't have said it, but as long as I am sticking my foot in my mouth this week, I thought, *Why not?* Tía Bertha is always talking shit, and here she is acting like she's perfect, criticizing me in front of everyone. Just because she's older than me she feels like she can keep doing this. Did I feel bad? Yes, of course I did, because I am Gabi Hernandez and feel bad about most decisions I make because lately those decisions have been bad ones. But, oh fucking well. I have had enough.

"I...well...uh..." She tried to respond. Beto was watching the whole scene unfold from the sofa. He just shook his head. Now he's judging me too? *Ugh*! First he's all, "I can't believe you got in a fight. What'd German do to anyone? He's a cool guy." And it takes all my strength not to shake him and tell him the truth. Now this.

"What, Beto?" I told him. "What did I do now?"

"Why'd you have to do that to tía Bertha? That was low."

"Why? Because she's always telling me how bad of a girl I am. How good girls do this and good girls do that. She doesn't even live by her own rules! She's screwing guys here and there and everywhere! Some of them are married. Making out in the street. She wants to wear pants, and I've seen her trying on make-up! She's such a hypocrite!" I was crying. Crying because I was angry. Crying because I felt guilty for calling my tía Bertha out. Crying because I probably lost my best friend. Crying because that's all I wanted to do.

"She's just..."

"Just what? She's mean! And I'm tired of it. The worst part of it, the worst part, Beto, is that she thinks she's bad. And she's not! She's just a normal person trying to be happy, but because she goes to that stupid church, and they fill her head with crazy ideas, she's miserable so she has to make everyone else miserable too. I don't get why she just can't be happy with who she is. No one is gonna think bad of her if she goes on dates or has sex or wears pants. Not even God."

He just stood there.

As I walked back to my room, I realized that tía Bertha had been standing in the hallway the whole time. Her head was in her hands and she was crying.

Hello, my name is Gabriela Hernandez, and I'm an asshole.

May 27

Things have been tense with tía Bertha. I felt bad when the guy in the red truck came by this morning and waited for tía Bertha to go out, and she never did. He eventually drove off as she watched him from the living room window. I asked her, "Why didn't you go out to see him?"

She didn't answer me. She won't even look at me.

I have gained like ten pounds these last few days, bingeing on junk food while I do my school work. By the time this week is over, I will probably have gained like 100 pounds and will have to be rolled onto the stage—if I do get to graduate after all.

Martin has texted me every day. He's upset because I won't tell him what German did either. Cindy is right—I should have stayed out of it. If I hadn't said anything, I would be at school stressing about graduation like everyone else—enjoying my last days as a senior, instead of being in isolation at home.

May 28

Today is Saturday. Graduation is in less than two weeks. Finals are done, and it would be time to celebrate except that I am the most miserable I have been in a long time. Sebastian came by today. He said that he couldn't believe I had violated Cindy's trust and that she was really upset. Though he said he understood why I did it and that he had felt like doing the same thing but stopped himself because of Cindy. He gave me a hug and said that he still loved me. But that it may take Cindy a while to forgive me. If she ever does.

May 30

Freedom! About midway through the afternoon, my school called and said that I wasn't suspended anymore and that I could come back to school tomorrow, but that I would have to go to the office first thing in the morning. Absolutely. Also, German dropped the charges. This was a bit confusing because he had no reason to. I kept asking myself all day what had happened. Maybe German realized that the truth would come out if he continued to go this route and that he would rather be the guy that got bitch-slapped by a girl than the guy who raped a girl. I don't know.

May 31

The good news: The principal told me that they were letting me come back to school because I had really good grades and had never been in trouble. She had done her investigation and realized that I had attacked German in self-defense, according to the witness she had spoken to. *Witness?* I thought. I bet it was the girl he was with, the one he had shoved to one side like she was nothing. In any case, I'll take it. The principal also said that she knew that I had been accepted to Berkeley and that she would make sure that this incident wouldn't go on any records that they would receive. *Whaaaaa?!* I was elated. The very very very bad news: I won't be able to walk during graduation. I felt a huge pain in my chest and even got a little dizzy. The principal said that she was sorry—she had pulled strings so this incident wouldn't be on my record, but that in exchange she had been asked that I not be allowed to walk like the other seniors who had gotten suspended. It was only fair, she said. That last rite of passage. That last step of being an American teenager—knocked out from under me. I had already bought my cap and gown. Family I hadn't seen in forever had been invited. This was going to be awful—one more reason my mom would have for calling me a bad girl. I left the office confused. I was so sad that I wouldn't walk, but I was happy that my admittance to Berkeley wasn't compromised. I needed Cindy and Sebastian. I had to talk to them about what happened. But I didn't get the chance to. I saw Martin first, and he was still mad because I wouldn't tell him the truth about why I was suspended, but he was happy I was back. His face dropped when I told him I wouldn't be able to walk, but he agreed with the principal.

"She's right, Gabi. It wouldn't be fair if you got to walk, and the other students didn't."

I wanted to shake him vigorously for saying that. I know it's the right thing to do! But why did he have to say it? Couldn't he have humored me for a bit and said, "That's so unfair!" No, he couldn't. That's not the kind of person Martin is.

Then I saw Cindy, and she was still angry at me so there would have been no sympathy there. Instead, I asked her if I could come see her after school to talk, and she said yes. Let's see how that goes.

Later...

I violated my friend's trust. She told me something in confidence that I had no right to share. What I should have done instead—and realized after researching on the internet (apparently a tool that can also be used for good, not just evil)—was to just be there for her and suggest she talk to someone (a teacher, the police, a counselor). I looked this info up before I went to her house and made a list of rape crisis hotline numbers and websites so that if she didn't want to talk to me anymore, she would have options.

When I got to her house, Cindy let me in, and we went to her room. She closed the door behind us.

"You know, Gabi, it was so hard for me to tell you what had happened. I didn't want anyone to know. I didn't. There are days I can't sleep, and I can't talk to boys because I'm afraid they'll do the same thing to me. Sometimes I cry for no reason, and then it all comes back. It happened to me. ME, Gabi. You didn't have a right to say anything."

Each word she said made me feel smaller and smaller and made me realize how much I had screwed up. "Cindy, I'm sorry. Nothing I say can make it right. I saw him with another girl and thought what if he does the same thing to her that he did to you? And before I knew it, I was on him, slapping the shit out of him. I was so angry that he didn't get punished and that he ruined your life. I know it was none of my business. And I hope you can forgive me."

She just shook her head. "I don't know. I know you were doing what you thought was right. Part of me is glad that you did it. He deserved it and more. But it doesn't change how I feel."

We sat and talked for hours. Cindy hadn't talked to anyone about how she felt. I mean she had told us what had happened but not how she felt. I had never seen her so sad, and I realized that it had been so hard for her to try to be "okay" in front of everyone. It was almost like she had been pretending. I gave her the list of hotlines I had made from my internet research and suggested she call one.

She said she was afraid, but I told her that some of them were anonymous and that they might be able to give her advice that would make her less afraid. We kept on talking until she changed the topic and said that she still loved me and that we were still friends. And that she was kind of glad that she had a friend who would always have her back in a slap fight. I couldn't help laughing at that. She said she was sorry I wouldn't be able to walk, but that it didn't mean that I couldn't go to the beach tomorrow for Senior Ditch Day. She's right. I might as well enjoy it. We can't be sad or mad forever.

June 1

Senior Ditch Day. Teachers and staff try and scare us by saying that we will be suspended or get detention for being absent. Yeah, they can't suspend over two hundred students—the school would lose all sorts of money, and they would have to spend all morning calling parents. We all decided to go to the beach. The sand was packed with teenagers trying to squeeze in the last moments of teenagehood. It was kind of weird being back after being suspended. People were staring at me and asking why I had hulked out on one of the hottest guys on campus. I was like, "I don't know. It all happened so fast." No one believed me, of course.

Cindy had said I could tell Martin what happened. When I told him, he was mad all over again and wanted to call the police. He said he didn't understand why Cindy was being so difficult and that she was just letting him go free. I told him what Cindy told me, "It happened to her, and she is dealing with it the best she can right now. I think she's going to get counseling, but all we can do is be there for her." Martin didn't really agree but said that he would respect her wishes.

It was early when we got to the beach, and some people were already there. The thing about being a fat girl is that bathing suits are at the top of your list of nightmares—along with diabetes, too-small leggings, pants that give you camel toe, underwires in a bra and a world without cheese. I had bought a two-piece suit a few weeks ago and had felt good about it. I tried it on and thought, "Gabi, you don't look like the cow you thought you looked like. You actually look good." And I had even given myself a thumbs up in the dressing room mirror. I have been running more often and had lost some weight, so everything was coming up Gabi. But then the whole German slapping incident happened, and I gained like five or ten pounds. The suit still fits but it's a little snugger than I had hoped. I had given myself the, "Who cares what other girls look like—you do you!" pep talk but this morning...*ugh*. I almost didn't want to go to the beach. Then I looked at myself in the mirror and read my poem for the week, a poem by Tracie Morris, "Project Princess." It's about a girl from the projects who doesn't care what people think about her—she just does what makes her feel confident. Then I looked myself straight in the eyes and said, "Gabi, get over it. You look spectacular. You look amazing, so stop your bitching or do something that makes you feel better." I took a deep breath and took off my shorts and shirt and stepped out on that beach like I owned that shit and didn't give a fuck about all the skinny girls around me. After a while, I didn't feel like an outsider and nobody made comments or even cared about what I looked like. The other thing about being fat is that you spend too much damn time worrying about being fat and that takes time away from having fun. But I decided today would be different. And it was.

By the afternoon, people were grilling and drinking and smoking weed—and some were even having sex in a small cove. Martin and I only walked into that super awkward situation because we were trying to find an empty part of the beach to talk for a bit. Okay—and maybe make out. But were we surprised when we found Debby Allen with Michael—from my physics class—totally going at it. Awkward. Michael gave us a thumbs up, and we just turned and walked away, laughing our asses off. The whole beach looked like a scene from a 1960s documentary. It was insane. I didn't partake in the drinking or smoking, but I definitely did eat. There was carne asada, burgers and hot dogs for days. When the sun started to go down, some people started making bonfires, but we had to take Cindy and Sabi (who her mom made her bring to the beach with her or else she couldn't go) home. We dropped them off hours ago and then went back to Martin's house since no one was home, and we had sex again. It was totally better this time around. I've been home for a few hours, and I can't go to sleep. Going to read a little bit. I started reading *East of Eden*, by John Steinbeck. It's a retelling of the Cain and Abel story from the Bible, and I am loving it. Steinbeck is a literary god. Oh my God, if I told Cindy or Sebastian that, they would never let me hear the end of it. I don't think Martin would let me live it down either.

June 2

I was sitting on the couch watching novelas with my mom and my tía when it hit me—these are the last few months I will be spending with them. I will miss them so much. I know my mom and I have our differences (she hates that I'm fat, I hate that she's controlling), but I love her with all my heart. Sure, she sneaks into my room and goes through my stuff, throwing away all my delicious snacks, looking for drugs or other evidence that I am being a bad daughter. But she has never found anything because I am a great daughter. And also great at hiding my precious treasures. Ha! But seriously,

I don't think I am as bad as she imagines me to be. She's just worried. She has been there for me when I've needed her the most, and I guess that balances things out. She's a walking contradiction—she wants me to be a strong woman and not let any man tell me what to do, but she also wants me to be obedient and behave like a nice young lady (whatever the hell that is): a virgin, I am sure, but what else? A good cook? A good reader? Someone who can make tortillas with one hand tied behind her back? Being a virgin can't be the only thing that makes you a "nice young lady" because I know plenty of girls who are virgins, but could never be called nice-young-anythings because they are straight-out spawn of Satan. But the untouched hymen is one of the requirements, my mother has insisted, that is inherently present in the anatomy of a nice young lady. She means well. It's probably hard for her to have been raised in some pueblo in the 1970s where being good at housework and being pure were seen as necessary traits for being married—because that is what you were supposed to aspire to do. So it's even harder (I'm guessing) to raise a Mexican-American daughter in Southern California in the 2000s, a girl who thinks that being good at housework and having an intact hymen are totally overrated. What is good anyway? I know that flourless espresso cake is good because it melts in my mouth, and I can't get enough of it. I know that carne asada tacos are good because my taste buds tell me so, and taste buds never lie.

But a good woman? A good girl? I have no clue.

I mean my tía tries her hardest to be a "good" Christian woman: long skirts and dresses, no make-up, no shoulders showing, no hair cutting and no worldly music. But she's not true to herself. And that can't be good. She loves worldly music, having sex, lipsticks, novelas and even wearing pants, but she won't give in because someone says that good women don't behave that way and—worse—that men don't want "those kinds" of women.

I would go crazy if I stayed here with them.

June 4

Hung out with Beto at the mall today. We ate some crappy Chinese food, bought some ugly T-shirt he wanted and ended up at the coffee shop where Martin and I have gone to read our poems. We sat and talked about so many things that we hadn't been able to, like my dad and Ernie and my mom. Beto says he feels guilty about saying he hated our dad, but that he's still mad at him for doing what he did.

I think Beto believes my dad overdosed on purpose.

Suicide.

It's something I've thought about—and even mentioned to Martin—

but I refuse to believe it. I don't want to think about that. It was an accident. That's all it was, no matter what Beto says. Beto and I talked about how crazy it is to have a little brother. For so long, it's just been us two and now—sixteen years later—there is someone new. Someone who we are responsible for in some way. We made a deal to not tell Ernie about what happened to our dad until he's out of high school. I don't know if that's realistic. I mean I am sure someone will someday tell him, "Oh, you're Ernie Hernandez? The kid whose dad was found dead in the garage." Why? Because our city is like that. Then Beto said something that made me cry.

"Gabi, when you leave, I'm going to miss fighting with you and you driving me around. I guess I'll have to find another chauffeur." This is brother speak for, "I'm going to miss you." And as soon as he saw me crying he was like, "Oh my God, Gabi. That's why I hate talking to you about shit. You always end up crying. Fuck."

I will so miss my brother.

June 5

Really missing my dad. The thing is that if my dad was still alive, I know that I would be more stressed out than I already am. It's not like he would be "here" in the present moment. Most likely he'd be high somewhere or high here at home. But still it would be nice to know that he's not becoming maggot food. There is this part of me that always felt like if I pleased my dad, if I gave him money, drove him to his friend's house, was extra nice to him, got good grades, I could have saved him. I know it's stupid and doesn't make sense, but I wish that's the way it would have worked. Sebastian says that you can't change people. "People are who they are no matter how much you want them to be somebody else, Gabi. And we have two choices: love and accept them with all their faults. Or not. In my case, my parents are choosing to not accept me because I can't change, and I won't pretend to be something I'm not. Your dad was an addict because that is what he wanted to be. There was nothing you could have done to change that." Sometimes Sebastian can be pretty deep.

June 6

My mom is so out of control! Is it so hard for her to understand that I want to move out? Today she told me that if I move out, I can't come back home—that if I leave, that's it. I can come to visit but not move back in. What am I supposed to do over the summer? She is trying so hard to keep me here, she doesn't realize that what she's doing is pushing me away.

She doesn't respect me as her daughter or as a person. All she wants is for me to be there whenever she wants me to be. But my needs? Ha! She could give a rat's ass about my needs. I don't care what she says. I don't. I'm leaving.

Later...

So my mom came in to talk to me and told me that I have to understand her. That she just wants what's best for me and that by me going so far away, I was playing with fire. "There are so many temptations out there, Gabi. What if you get pregnant? What if they offer you drugs? Here at least I can keep an eye on you. ¿Pero allá?"

I grew some and told her that if I wanted to have sex, I could do it here. That I have already been offered drugs, and I have said no. That she raised a semi-decent daughter that she could trust. And that I was moving out and that I would love her support, but either way I had to go. I hate making my mom cry.

But I think she may have understood because before she left my room she said, "Pues, esta siempre es tu casa." Which was really all I needed to hear. I knew she had been bluffing.

June 8

If anyone were to visit our high school right now, they would think that someone had died with all the crying and hugging that is going on. And it's pretty lame because people have each other's phone numbers and if they're your friends, you probably see them on the weekends or after school anyway. I tried to understand it. Martin says it's because for a lot of people, high school is it—the best time of their life. Oh my God, if high school is supposed to be the best time of my life, I'm going to have the shittiest life ever. I can't imagine thinking this is it. That this is my peak. I'd rather think, *Finally, it's over*. But no. Everywhere people are emotional train wrecks. I guess I get it. It's a rite of passage, like getting your period. Except that with leaving high school, I feel that I won't be rolling around on the ground because of the near-death experience that is cramps. I hope to sweet baby Jesus that's not what it will be like. I hope that it's more like other rites of passage, like sex—it's uncomfortable getting through it the first time, but then it's not.

I do have to say I will miss Ms. Abernard, who has been giving us poems about overcoming adversity. My favorite one so far has been, "Still I Rise" by Maya Angelou.

June 12

Today would have been the day I walked across the stage wearing my cap and gown with the rest of my class. Instead, I am the person waiting at Pepe's House of Wings, reserving the table for ten. As it turns out when you are suspended from school for slapping the crap out of a rapist, you are forbidden to participate in any way—even as an audience member—in any school activities. This meant I couldn't even watch my friends cross the stage. I was so freaking mad, but I kept reminding myself that at least I could still go to Berkeley (with Martin, of course, because that super smart boyfriend of mine got in too!) and that was the most important thing.

But there was no way in hell I would pass up Pepe's House of Wings for anything—I mean Eric works here, and I still show up. As I sat there salivating, thinking of the wings to come, my eyes wandered out the window to a red pickup truck that looked familiar. The passenger door opened and who should come out but my tía Bertha! Wearing Satan's clothing: pants and a short-sleeved blouse! Her hair had been cut and— the topper—she had on bright pink lipstick! Tía Bertha in public with a man? *Is it the end of days?* I thought. *Should I duck and cover?* I tried to hold it together when she came in, but was close to losing my shit when she INTRODUCED him to me.

"Gabi, this is Raul. Raul, this is my niece Gabi. The one I told you about who is going to college."

Holy moly. I could barely shake his hand. I bet my eyes were super wide because tía Bertha asked if I was okay. I squeaked out a, "Yeah."

Raul went to the bathroom, and I asked tía Bertha, "Pants? Lipstick? ¿Y su pelo? What's going on, tía?"

"Gabi, the other day you made me think about my life. You may not know this, but I like men."

I almost spit out my lemonade. Everyone knows that.

"And,"—she didn't miss a beat—"I have been lonely. When your father died, I didn't know what to do. I felt like I had failed God and that is why my brother died. Like God was punishing me because of my love for men. But then I realized that it had nothing to do with me. That my brother was sick and had chosen his path the day he first picked up that pipe, and that there was probably very little I could have done to help him. I got mad at God, Gabi. It was a very confusing time, and that's why I left. When I came back, I only pretended to be happy. When you said those things about being a "good girl" and hurt my feelings, I realized it wasn't worth it. Living a lie is painful and doesn't do anyone any good. I had to be true to myself, because either way God would know if I was lying."

If at the beginning at the school year, someone had said, "Gabi, I am coming from the future to tell you that you will not walk across the stage on graduation day but instead you will be chillaxing at Pepe's House of Wings with your tía Bertha and her boyfriend," I would have laughed in their face and told them to stop smoking that reefer. But it happened, and it wasn't as weird as I thought it would be (okay, it was pretty weird). We talked for a while and when her boyfriend came back, I learned that he works in construction and on weekends sells tacos outside a liquor store in Stuffix (I tried not to show how excited I was at the prospect of getting an unlimited supply of free tacos, but I think he saw through me). The way my tía looks at Raul is the way I look at Martin. He makes her happy and helps her see that she is stronger than she thought she was. It's not that he makes her stronger, but he definitely helps her see that she has been strong all along.

Martin was the first one to pull up. He had brought me some flowers (what a nerd). As soon as he walked in, he gave me a kiss on the cheek and went to order some lemon pepper wings. We truly do make a beautiful couple. Not long after, everyone else arrived. My mom and Beto—with Ernie in his arms—got there, arguing about why she should let him go camping with his friends for a whole week. She'll probably give in later. Cindy and Sebastian pulled up, still wearing their caps and gowns, of course, bumping some super loud music, letting everyone know just how excited they were. I won't lie, I still feel pretty shitty about not being able to walk with my class—I feel like I let myself down—but seeing my beautifully crazy and colorful all-American family sit together at a slightly sticky table in one of the best hot wing restaurants in all the land, in a rundown shopping strip, made me feel like everything was as it should be, and that all the things I am worried about are gonna be all right.

And if anyone has trouble understanding that, well, they can kiss my ass.

Acknowledgments

First, I'd like to say thank you to Cinco Puntos Press. Third time's the charm. Especially to Lee for all her expertise that has made this book so much stronger and better. The Byrds and the rest of Cinco Puntos—Jessica, Mary, and the various interns including Amber—believed in Gabi and gave us a chance. I am forever grateful for all of their support these last five years. Thank you still seems insufficient, but it is still all I have.

Thank you to Zeke Peña who designed the amazing cover. I love it so much still. You've been an amazing collaborator and have helped me grow so much as a writer, and you've been a great friend.

Thank you to all my teachers, especially Ms. Brenda Agard who made us memorize e.e. cummings' "anyone lived in a pretty how town" in tenth grade and changed my life forever. And also thanks to: Ms. Edie Sonnenburg (thanks for paying for my SATs and ACTs); Ms. Schneider (for telling me I was the best reader in the class); Mrs. Osti (for making reading magical); Mr. Alford (for giving me that collection of *Goosebumps* that Christmas we got the basket); Ms. Beverly Siddons (for making us think and think and think); Ms. Marilyn Erdei (for telling me that my study habits would never change and I couldn't be in AP English); Ms. Linda Laing (who made school fun); Dr. Ellen Gil-Gomez (who's just awesome and always supportive); Dr. Julie Paegle (who suggested I take this writing thing seriously); and Dr. Jackie Rhodes (for being a bad ass).

Thank you to PoetrIE—my writing family. I am forever indebted to you for your constant encouragement, high fives, "that's not working," "keep submitting," "keep submitting," and friendship: Larry Eby, Jason E. Keller, Aaron Reeder, Mouse, and Cherie Rouse, you guys are freaking amazing. But to poet/artist/former hippie and sometimes roommate Cindy Rinne, thank you for taking the time to read and comment on this book more than once. To Connie Lopez-Hood, amazing poet, kind soul, and daughter of the universe. Thank you for your revisions, always kind words, and honesty when things didn't make sense.

To Elisa Grajeda-Urmston, for looking things over, and boosting my ego.

Thank you Angela Asbell for one day, long, long ago, explaining to me what a zine was.

Thank you to Micah Chatterton for listening.

To Gaby Littler for being excited twelve years ago when I showed you the early early draft.

And huge thank you to Orlando Ramirez for helping make Gabi a poet.

Gracias to the baddest Chicana role model of them all, the late, great, Michele Serros for her work and advice.

A big thank you to my ex-husband, my ex-in-laws, and nieces and nephews for their support. There are way too many to list.

To my Trapp family—all the teachers, staff, and parents who encouraged me, gracias. Especially to Linda Stoll—my Lindy Lou.

To Maggie Coates for giving me the thumbs up.

To my hermanas—April, Amanda, Dow, Lety, Rita, Lauron, Karina, Vanessa, Ofelia, and Mary Ann. You guys were right, si se puede.

Thanks to Eli Cornelius and Chrysta Wong-Sierra for always keepin' it real. Always.

To Lisha, for EVERYTHING. To Juan Bahena for answering ALL my interesting questions. To Lupita, Ana, Ruth, and Mago for always believing.

Thanks to all the readers, educators, booksellers, bloggers, and everyone else who has used Gabi in their classes, dissertations, presentations, or who has recommended it. Thank you to Belen, Amanda, Pável, Alejandro, Cati, Allyson, Chance , Sarah, Cellar Door Books, Casandra, Erika: your belief in me and my work is something I hope everyone has. And to all my new author friends, I love you all.

Thank you to Lupe y Victor, my parents, who love and support me. Especially my mom who has never once doubted my potential or the possibilities that I carry. Thanks to my brother who always has my back.